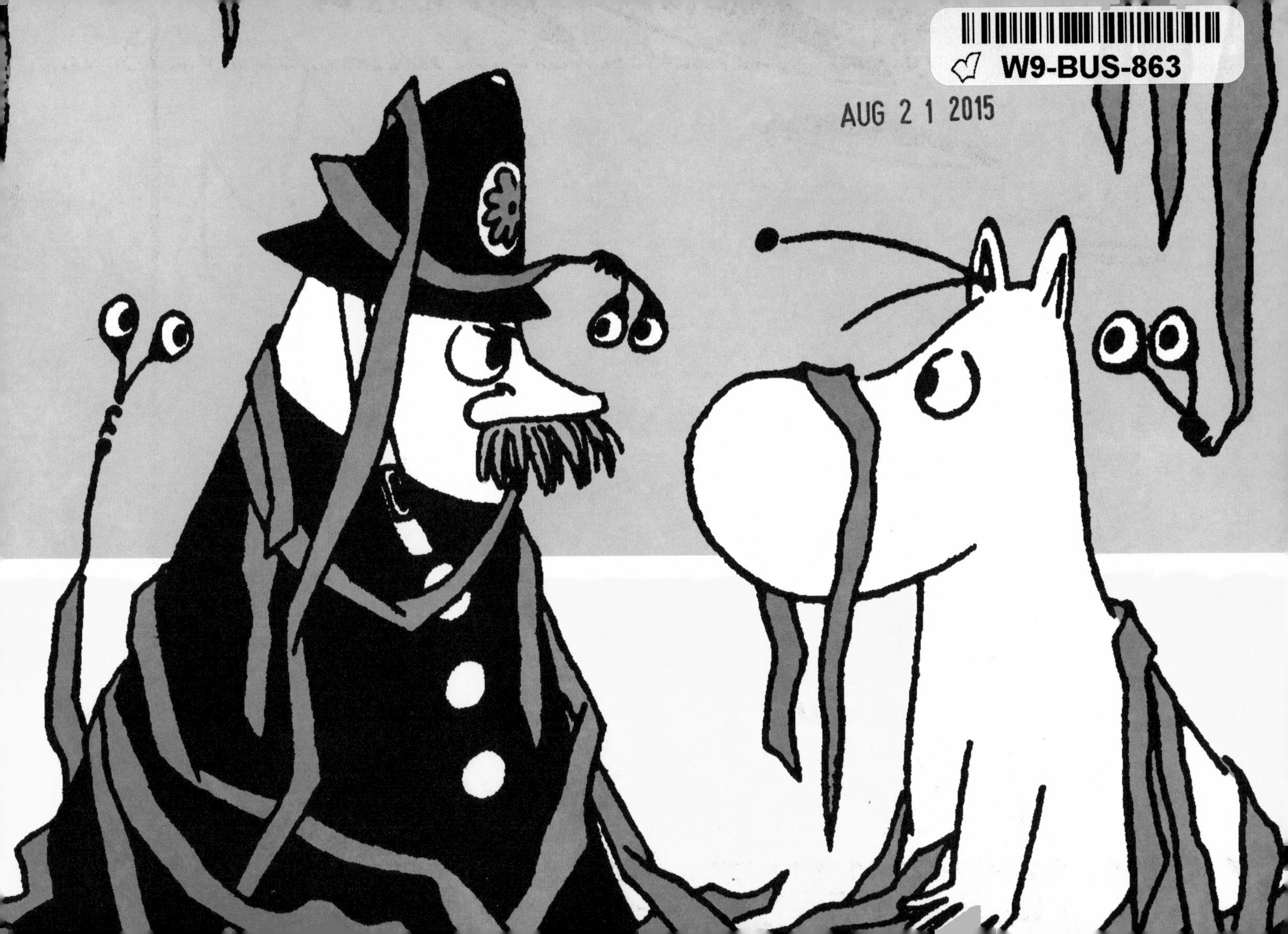

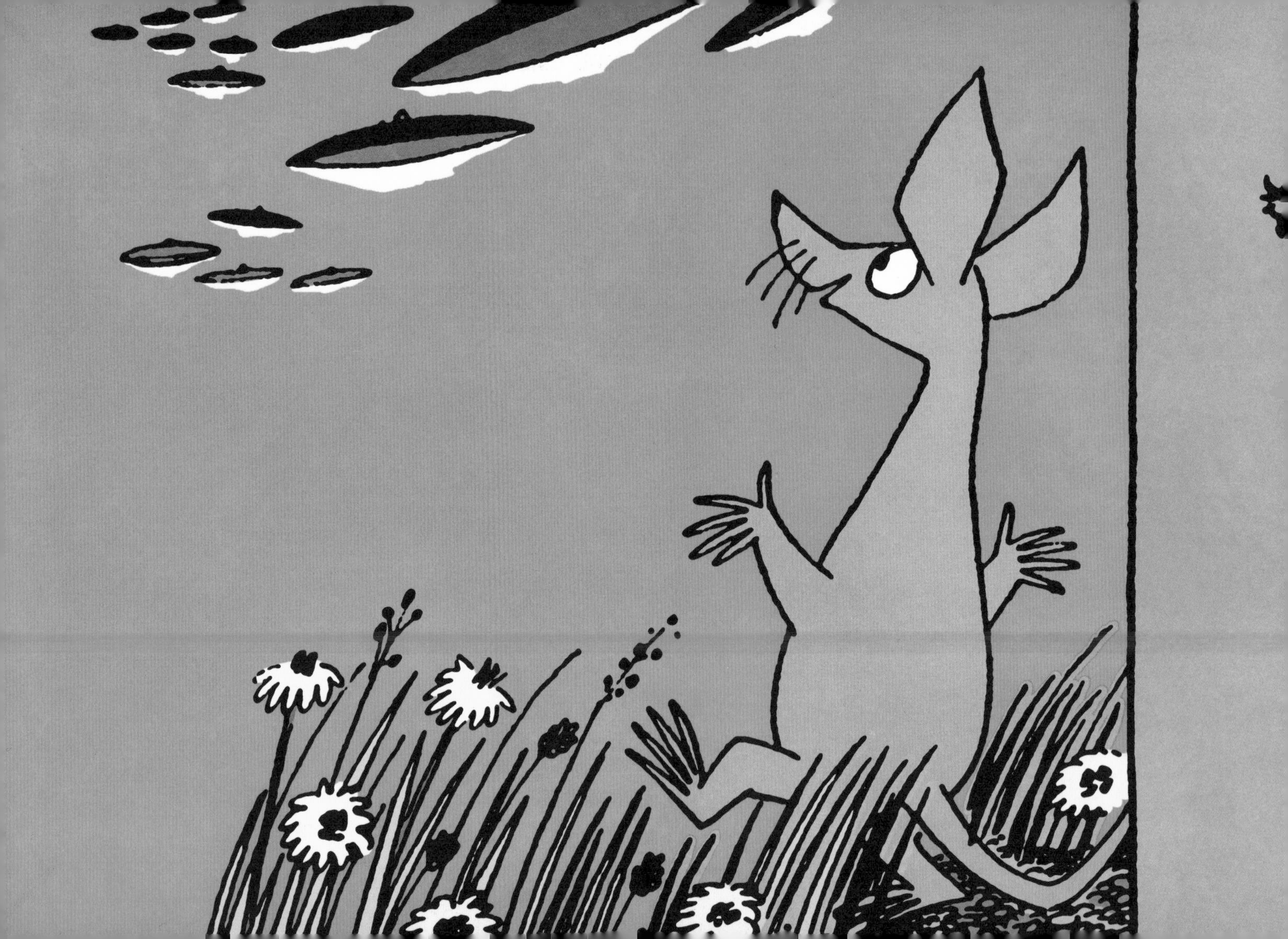

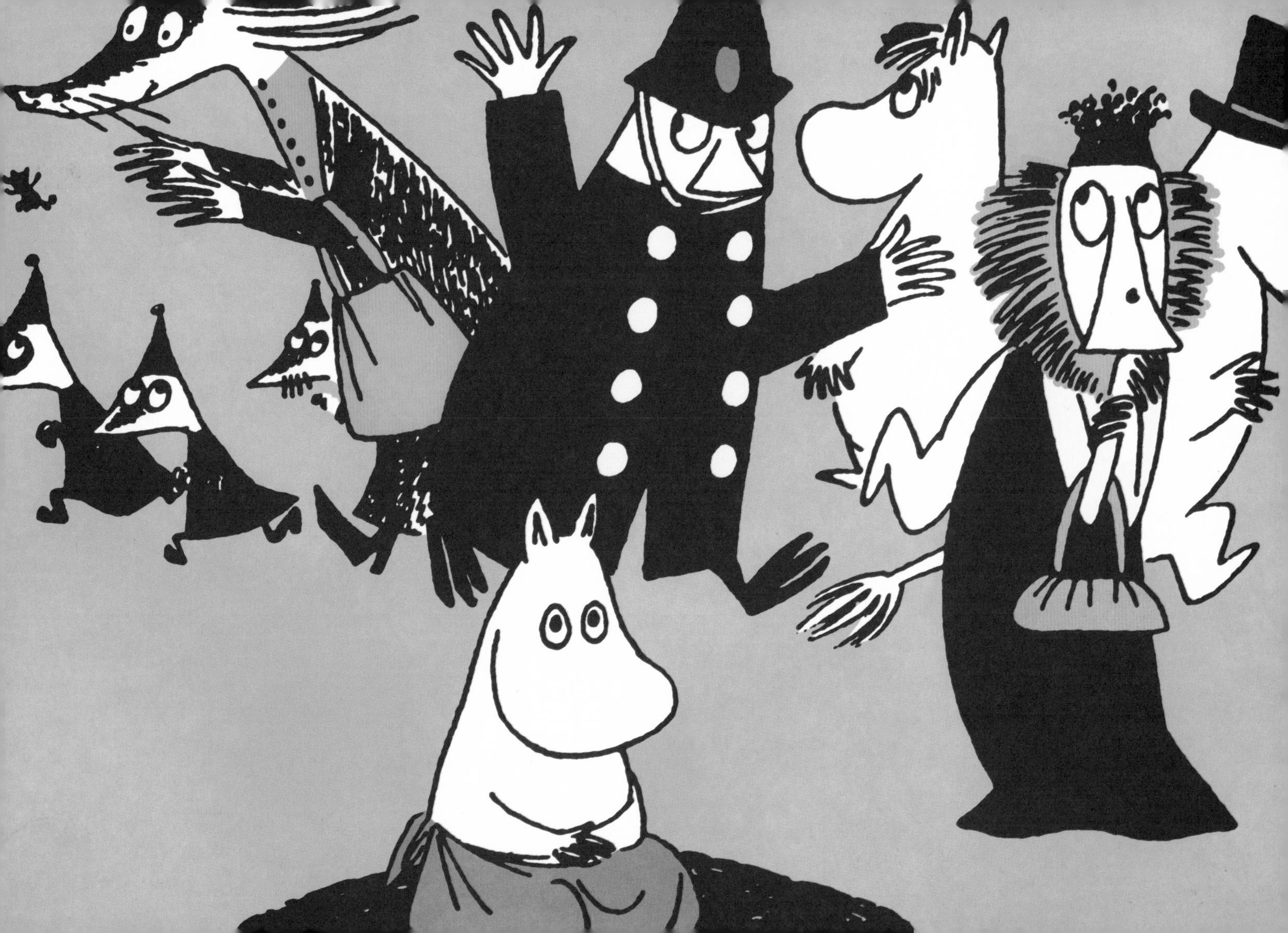

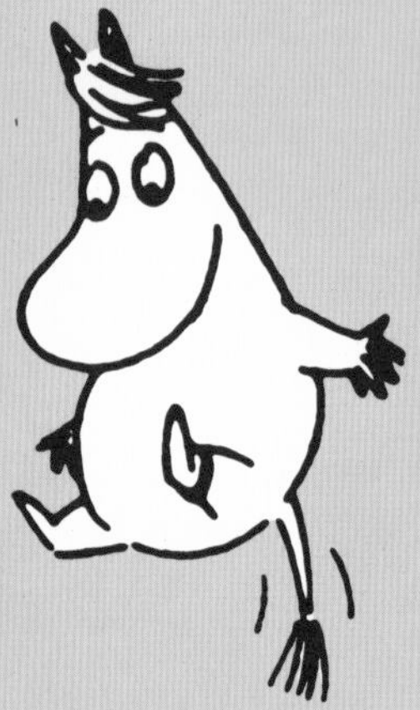

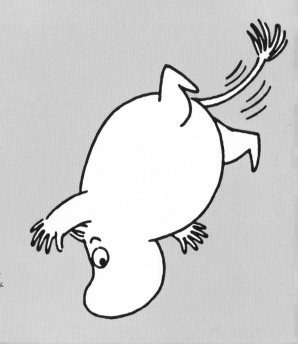

Library and Archives Canada Cataloguing in Publication
Jansson, Tove, author, illustrator
Moomin and the Martians/Tove Jansson.
A selection from the Moomin comic strip series originally published in the British newspaper, the Evening news (1957).
ISBN 978-1-77046-203-8 (pbk.)
1. Comic books, strips, etc. I. Title.
PZ7.7.J35MOM 2015   J741.5'94897   C2014-907026-8

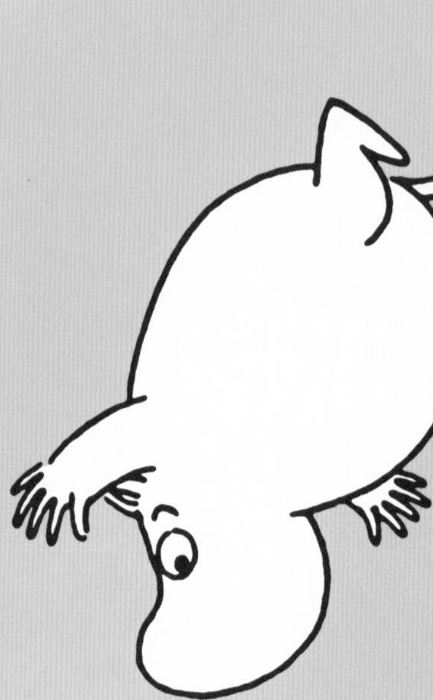

Published in the USA by Enfant,
a client publisher of Farrar, Straus and Giroux
Orders: 888.330.8477

Published in Canada by Enfant,
a client publisher of Raincoast Books
Orders: 800.663.5714

Published in the United Kingdom by Enfant,
a client publisher of Publishers Group UK
Orders: info@pguk.co.uk

Enfant is an imprint of Drawn & Quarterly.

drawnandquarterly.com

First edition: August 2015
Printed in Malaysia
10 9 8 7 6 5 4 3 2 1

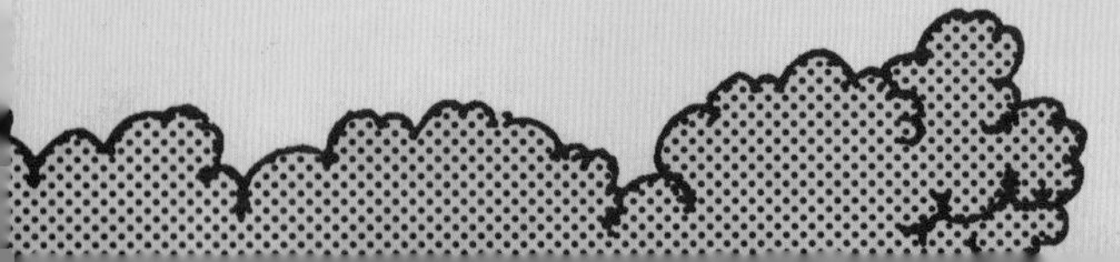

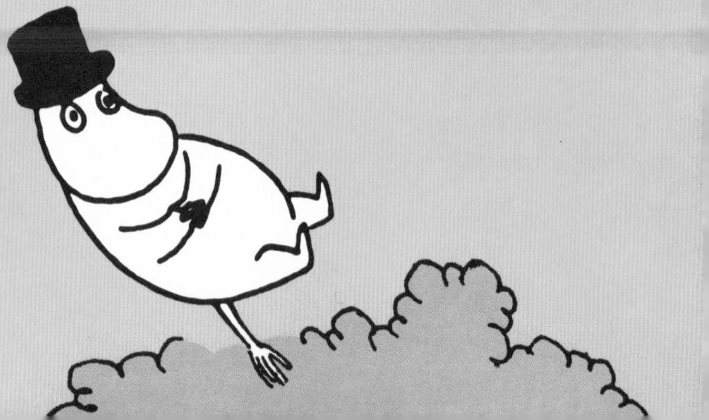

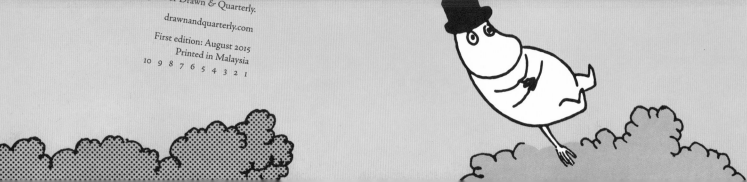

MOOMIN AND THE MARTIANS

Tove Jansson

ENFANT

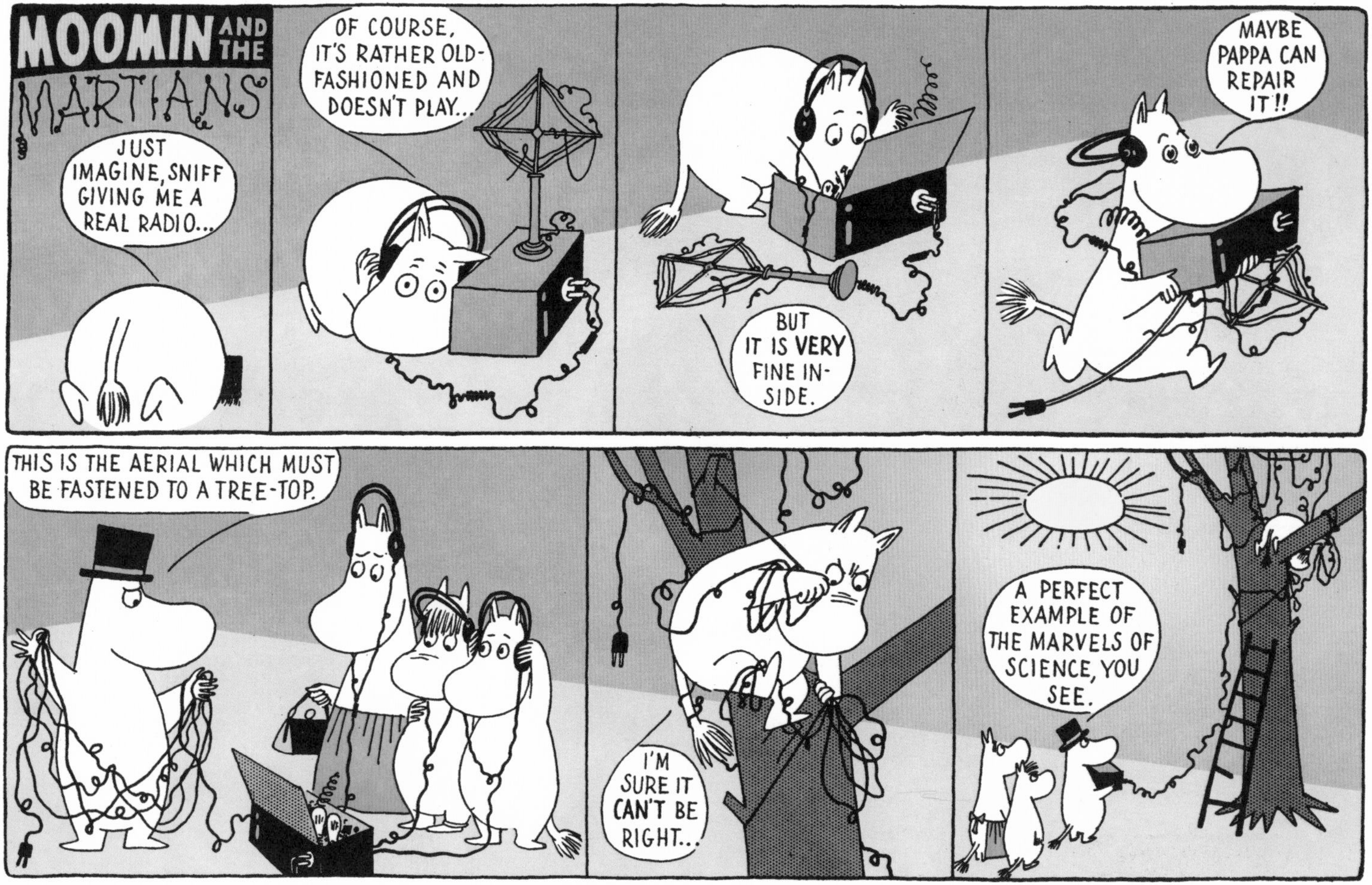
MOOMIN AND THE MARTIANS
JUST IMAGINE, SNIFF GIVING ME A REAL RADIO...
OF COURSE, IT'S RATHER OLD-FASHIONED AND DOESN'T PLAY...
BUT IT IS VERY FINE IN-SIDE.
MAYBE PAPPA CAN REPAIR IT!!
THIS IS THE AERIAL WHICH MUST BE FASTENED TO A TREE-TOP.
I'M SURE IT CAN'T BE RIGHT...
A PERFECT EXAMPLE OF THE MARVELS OF SCIENCE, YOU SEE.

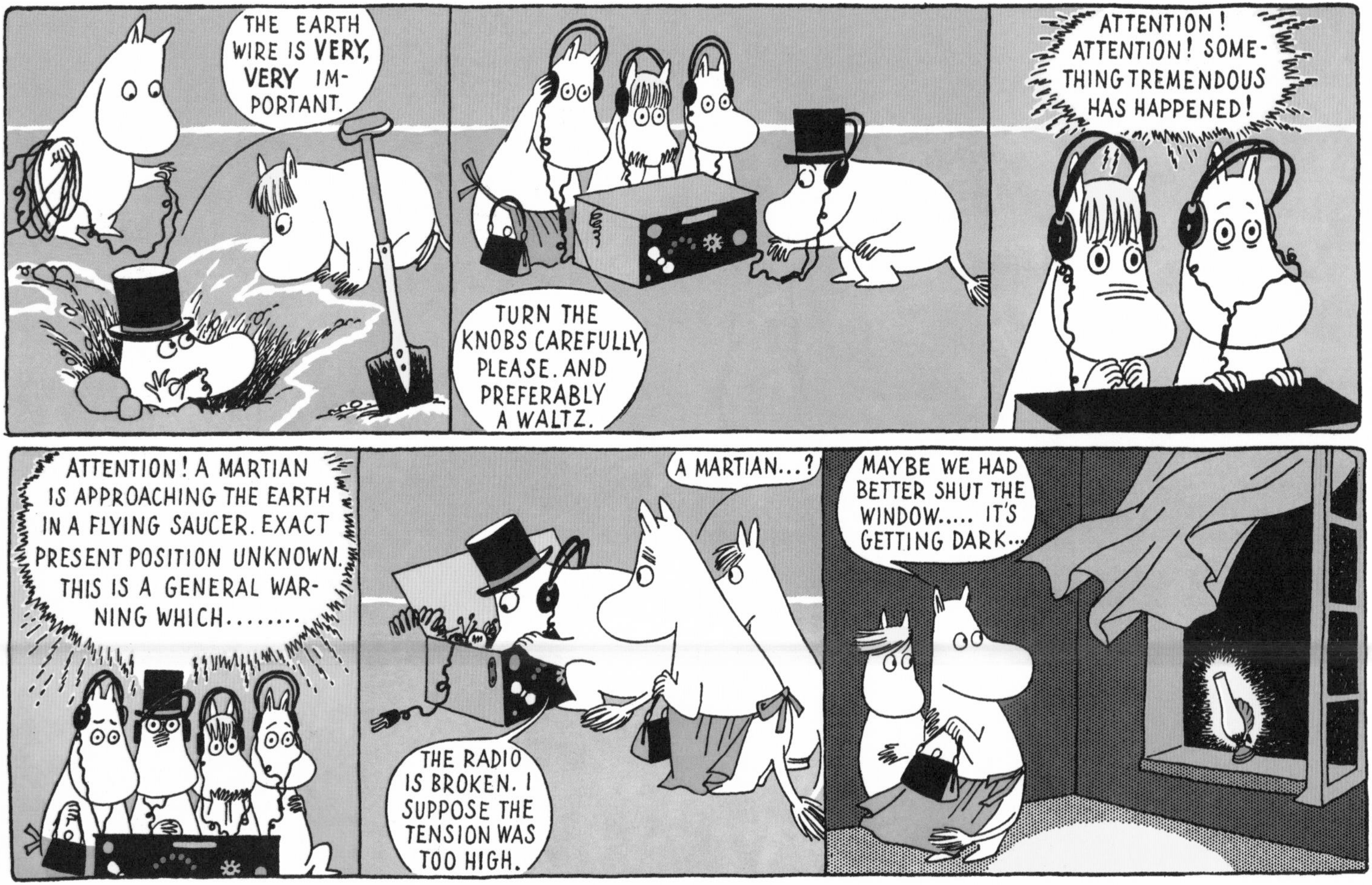
THE EARTH WIRE IS VERY, VERY IMPORTANT.
TURN THE KNOBS CAREFULLY, PLEASE. AND PREFERABLY A WALTZ.
ATTENTION! ATTENTION! SOMETHING TREMENDOUS HAS HAPPENED!
ATTENTION! A MARTIAN IS APPROACHING THE EARTH IN A FLYING SAUCER. EXACT PRESENT POSITION UNKNOWN. THIS IS A GENERAL WARNING WHICH........
A MARTIAN...?
THE RADIO IS BROKEN. I SUPPOSE THE TENSION WAS TOO HIGH.
MAYBE WE HAD BETTER SHUT THE WINDOW..... IT'S GETTING DARK...

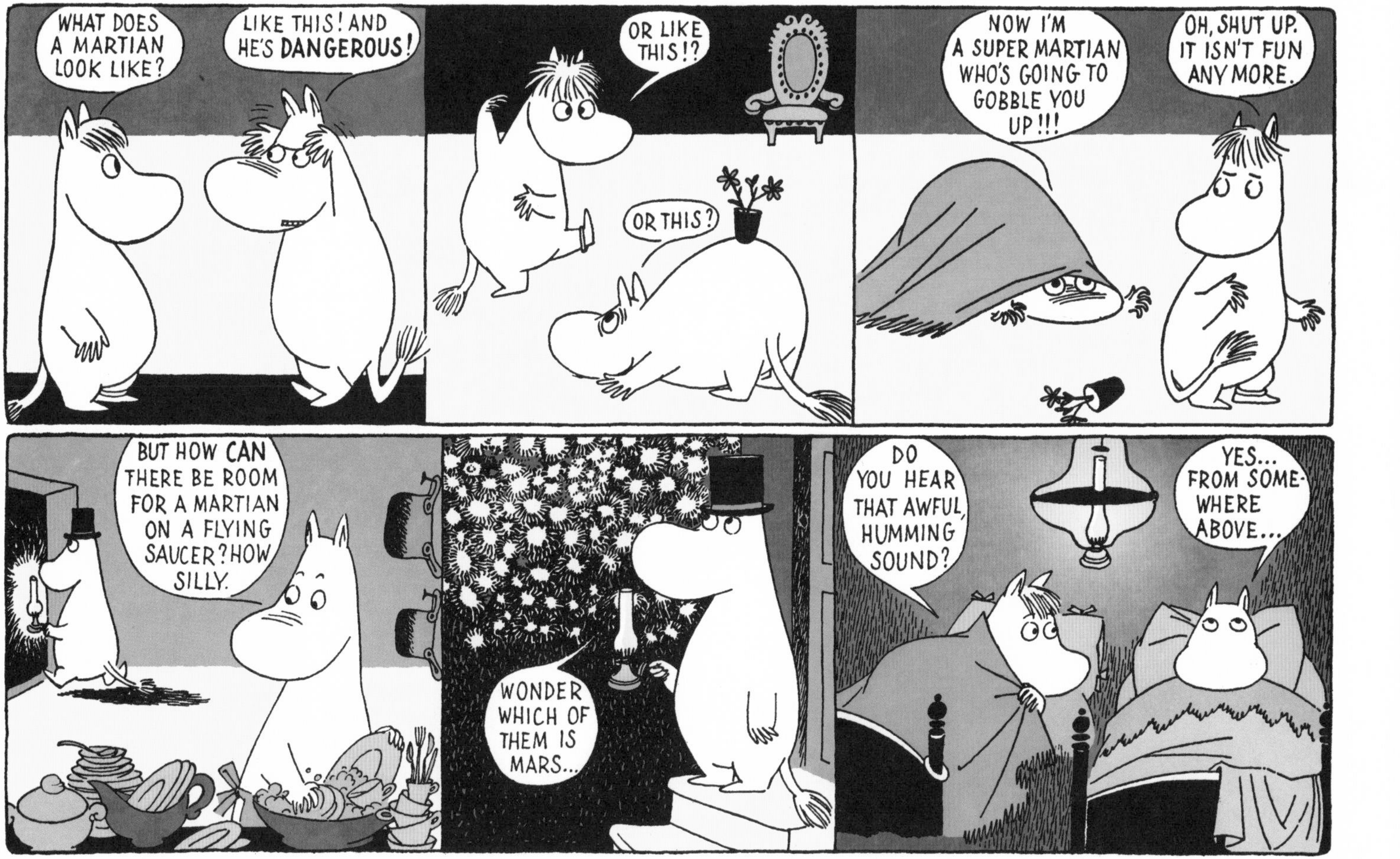
WHAT DOES A MARTIAN LOOK LIKE?
LIKE THIS! AND HE'S DANGEROUS!
OR LIKE THIS!?
OR THIS?
NOW I'M A SUPER MARTIAN WHO'S GOING TO GOBBLE YOU UP!!!
OH, SHUT UP. IT ISN'T FUN ANY MORE.
BUT HOW CAN THERE BE ROOM FOR A MARTIAN ON A FLYING SAUCER? HOW SILLY.
WONDER WHICH OF THEM IS MARS...
DO YOU HEAR THAT AWFUL, HUMMING SOUND?
YES... FROM SOMEWHERE ABOVE...

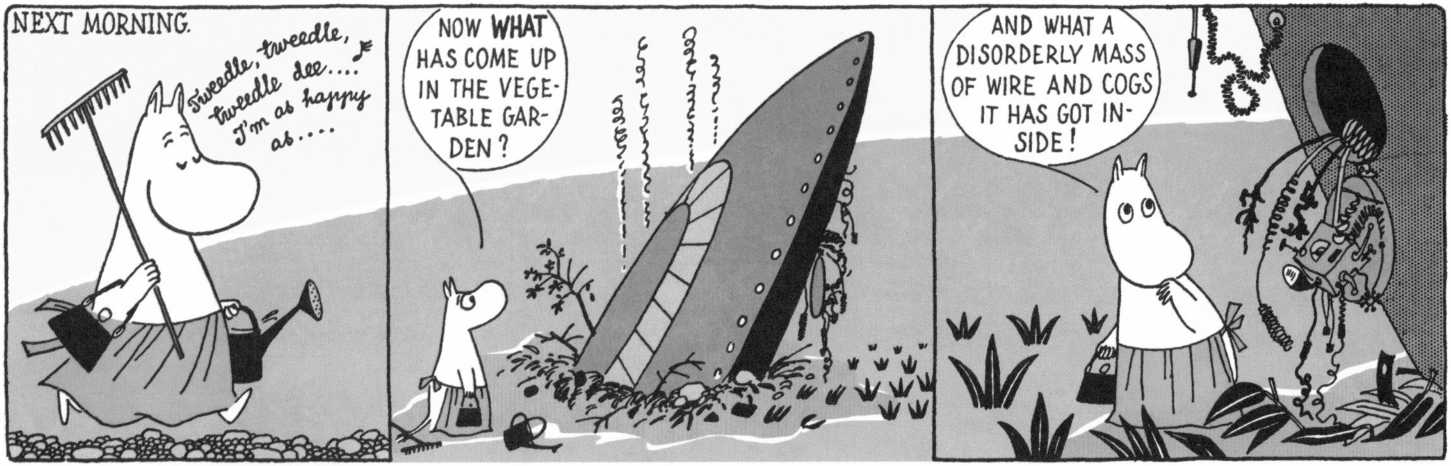
NEXT MORNING.
Tweedle, tweedle, tweedle dee.... I'm as happy as....
NOW WHAT HAS COME UP IN THE VEGETABLE GARDEN?
AND WHAT A DISORDERLY MASS OF WIRE AND COGS IT HAS GOT INSIDE!

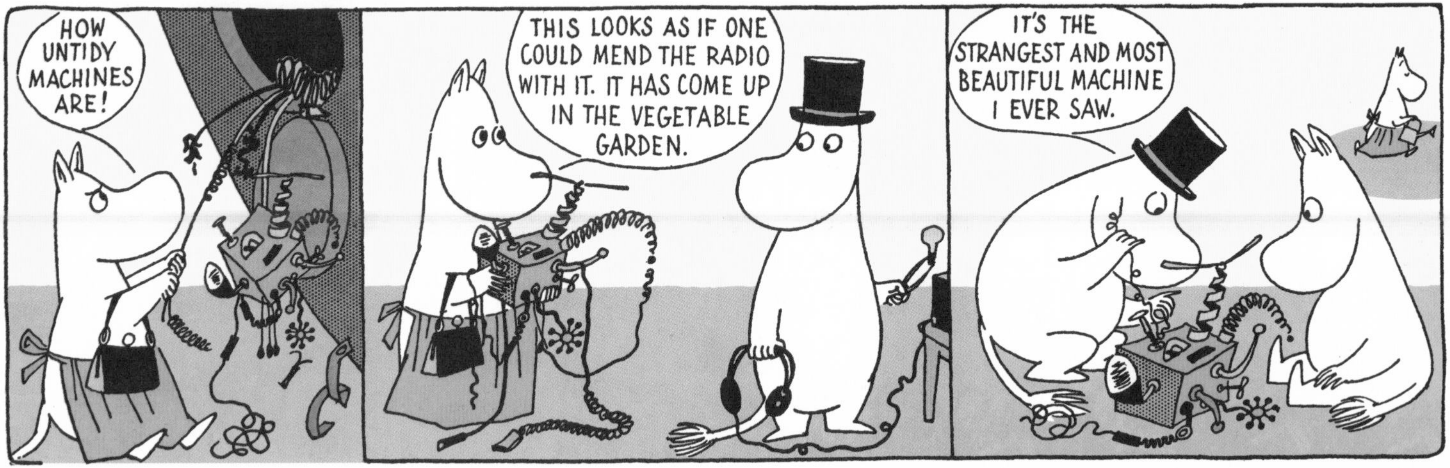
HOW UNTIDY MACHINES ARE!
THIS LOOKS AS IF ONE COULD MEND THE RADIO WITH IT. IT HAS COME UP IN THE VEGETABLE GARDEN.
IT'S THE STRANGEST AND MOST BEAUTIFUL MACHINE I EVER SAW.

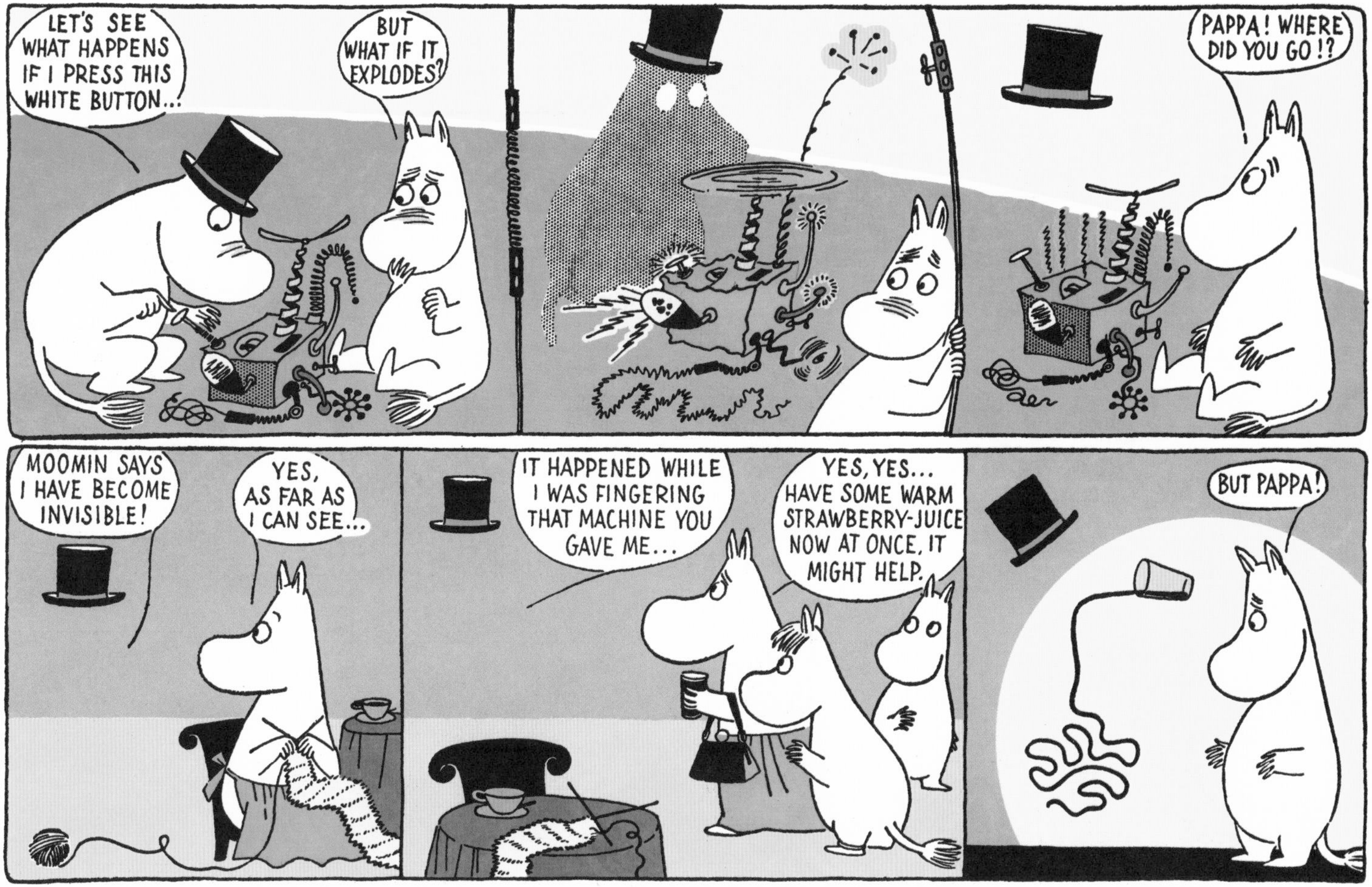
LET'S SEE WHAT HAPPENS IF I PRESS THIS WHITE BUTTON...
BUT WHAT IF IT EXPLODES?
PAPPA! WHERE DID YOU GO!?
MOOMIN SAYS I HAVE BECOME INVISIBLE!
YES, AS FAR AS I CAN SEE...
IT HAPPENED WHILE I WAS FINGERING THAT MACHINE YOU GAVE ME...
YES, YES... HAVE SOME WARM STRAWBERRY-JUICE NOW AT ONCE, IT MIGHT HELP.
BUT PAPPA!

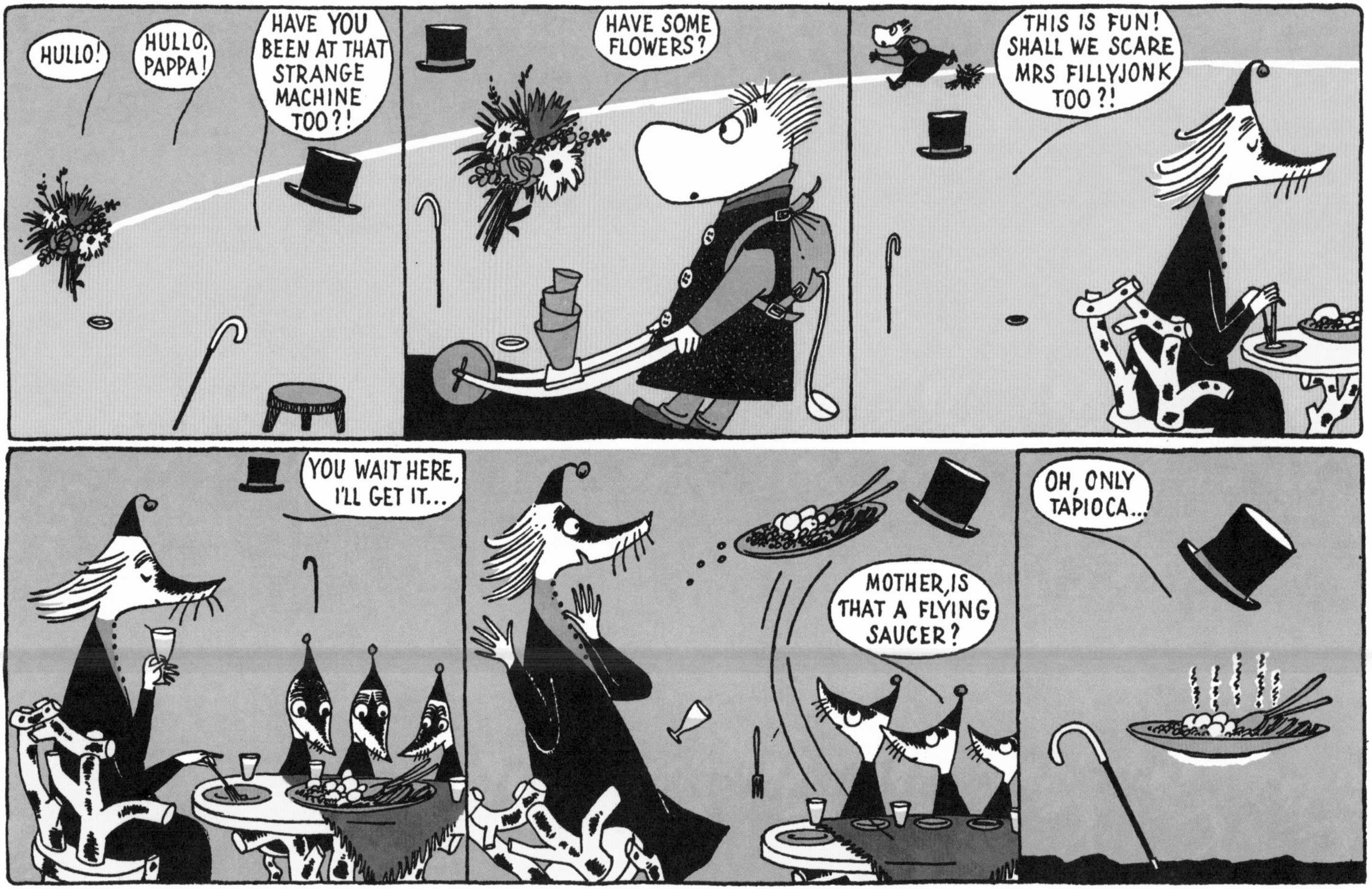
HULLO!
HULLO, PAPPA!
HAVE YOU BEEN AT THAT STRANGE MACHINE TOO?!
HAVE SOME FLOWERS?
THIS IS FUN! SHALL WE SCARE MRS FILLYJONK TOO?!
YOU WAIT HERE, I'LL GET IT...
MOTHER, IS THAT A FLYING SAUCER?
OH, ONLY TAPIOCA...

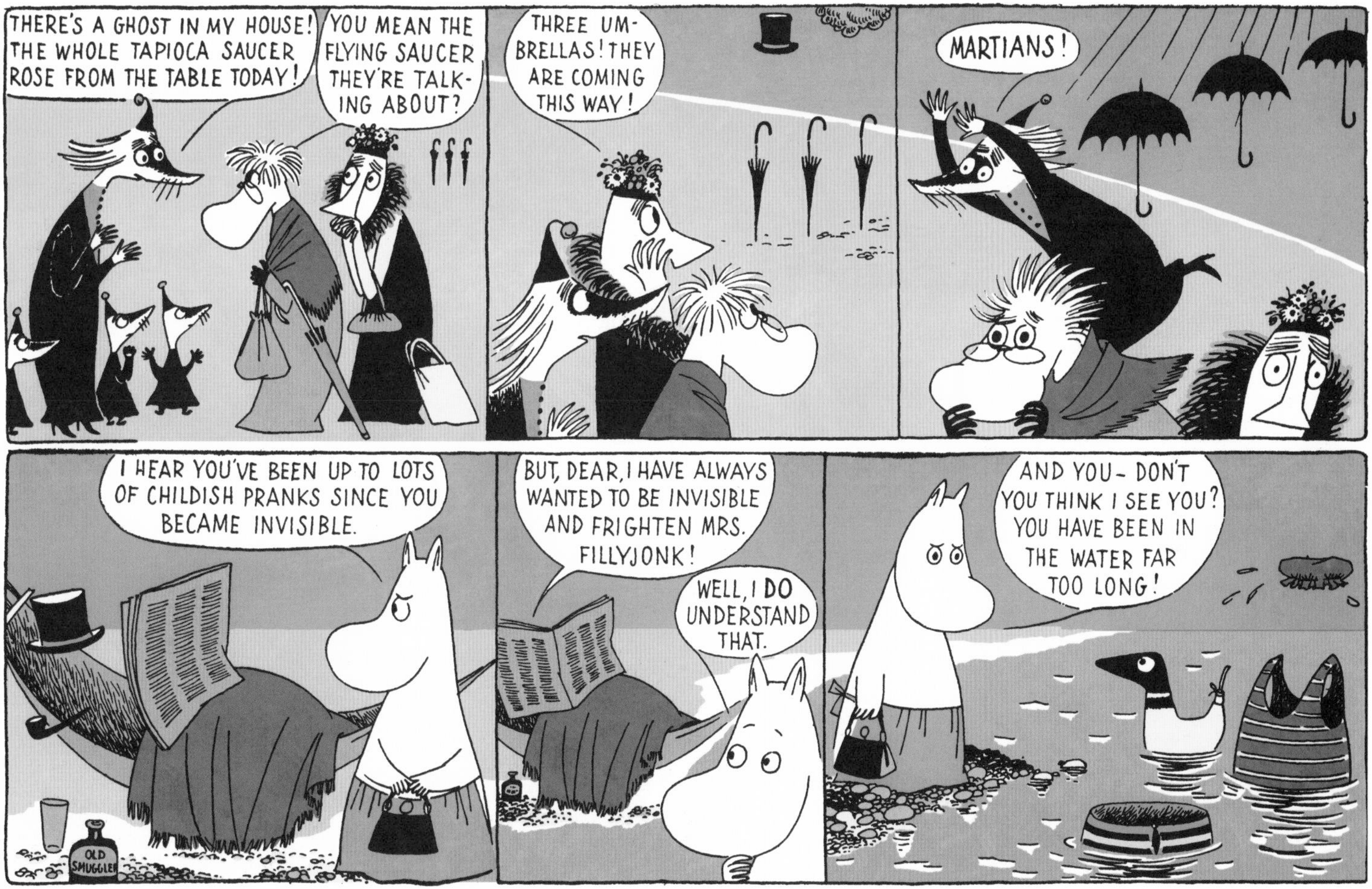
THERE'S A GHOST IN MY HOUSE! THE WHOLE TAPIOCA SAUCER ROSE FROM THE TABLE TODAY!
YOU MEAN THE FLYING SAUCER THEY'RE TALKING ABOUT?
THREE UMBRELLAS! THEY ARE COMING THIS WAY!
MARTIANS!
I HEAR YOU'VE BEEN UP TO LOTS OF CHILDISH PRANKS SINCE YOU BECAME INVISIBLE.
OLD SMUGGLER
BUT, DEAR, I HAVE ALWAYS WANTED TO BE INVISIBLE AND FRIGHTEN MRS. FILLYJONK!
WELL, I **DO** UNDERSTAND THAT.
AND YOU - DON'T YOU THINK I SEE YOU? YOU HAVE BEEN IN THE WATER FAR TOO LONG!

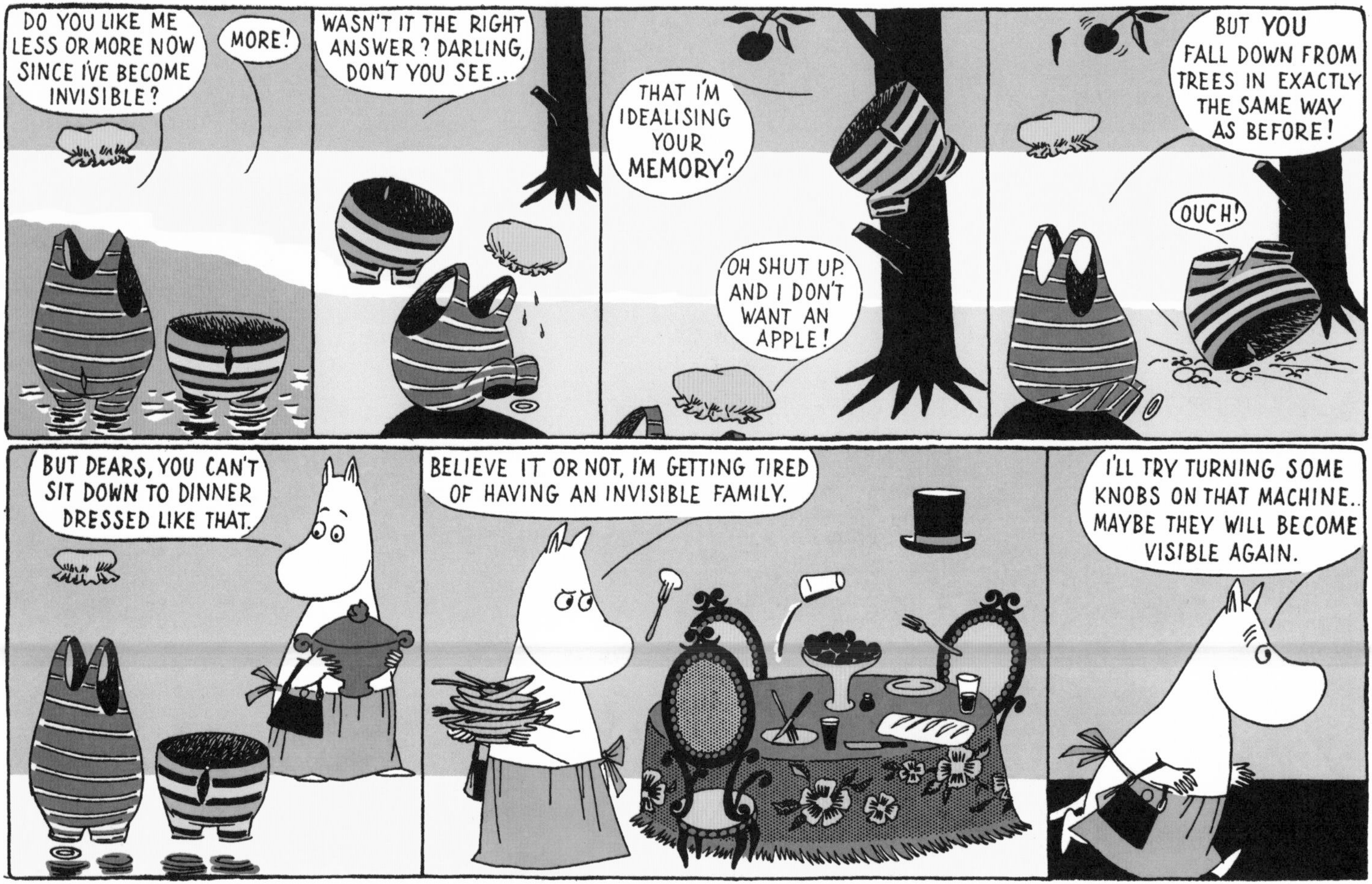
DO YOU LIKE ME LESS OR MORE NOW SINCE I'VE BECOME INVISIBLE?
MORE!
WASN'T IT THE RIGHT ANSWER? DARLING, DON'T YOU SEE...
THAT I'M IDEALISING YOUR MEMORY?
OH SHUT UP. AND I DON'T WANT AN APPLE!
BUT YOU FALL DOWN FROM TREES IN EXACTLY THE SAME WAY AS BEFORE!
OUCH!
BUT DEARS, YOU CAN'T SIT DOWN TO DINNER DRESSED LIKE THAT.
BELIEVE IT OR NOT, I'M GETTING TIRED OF HAVING AN INVISIBLE FAMILY.
I'LL TRY TURNING SOME KNOBS ON THAT MACHINE.. MAYBE THEY WILL BECOME VISIBLE AGAIN.

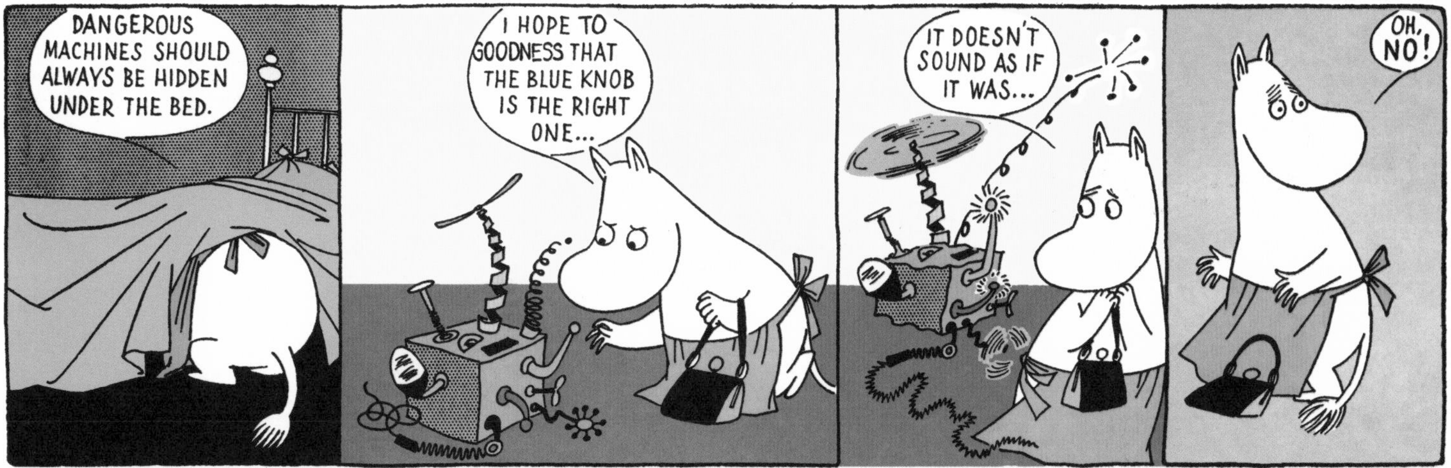
DANGEROUS MACHINES SHOULD ALWAYS BE HIDDEN UNDER THE BED.
I HOPE TO GOODNESS THAT THE BLUE KNOB IS THE RIGHT ONE...
IT DOESN'T SOUND AS IF IT WAS...
OH, NO!

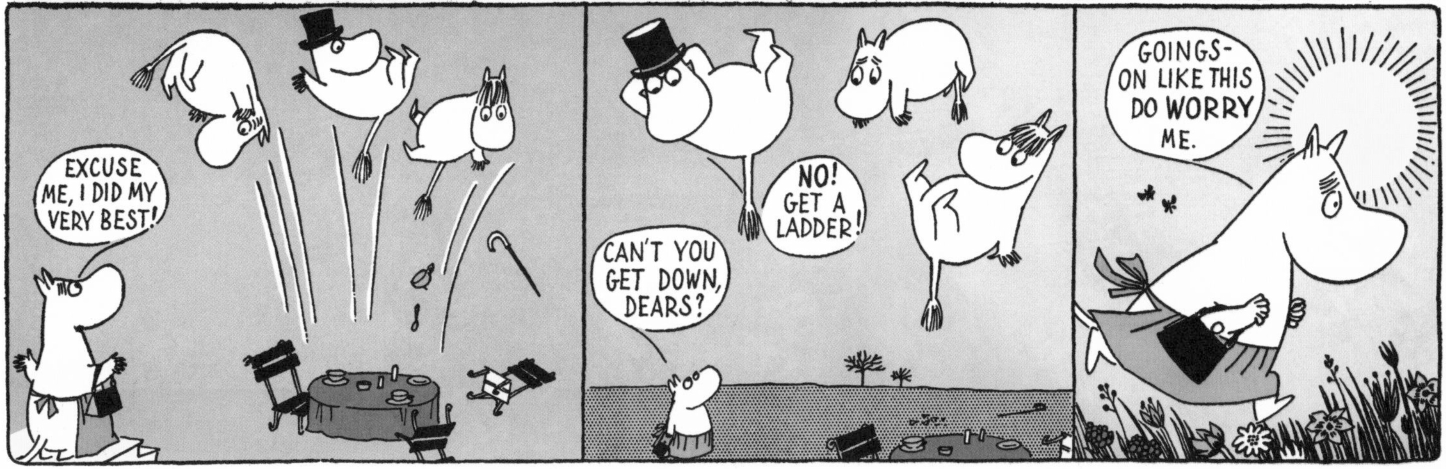
EXCUSE ME, I DID MY VERY BEST!
CAN'T YOU GET DOWN, DEARS?
NO! GET A LADDER!
GOINGS-ON LIKE THIS DO WORRY ME.

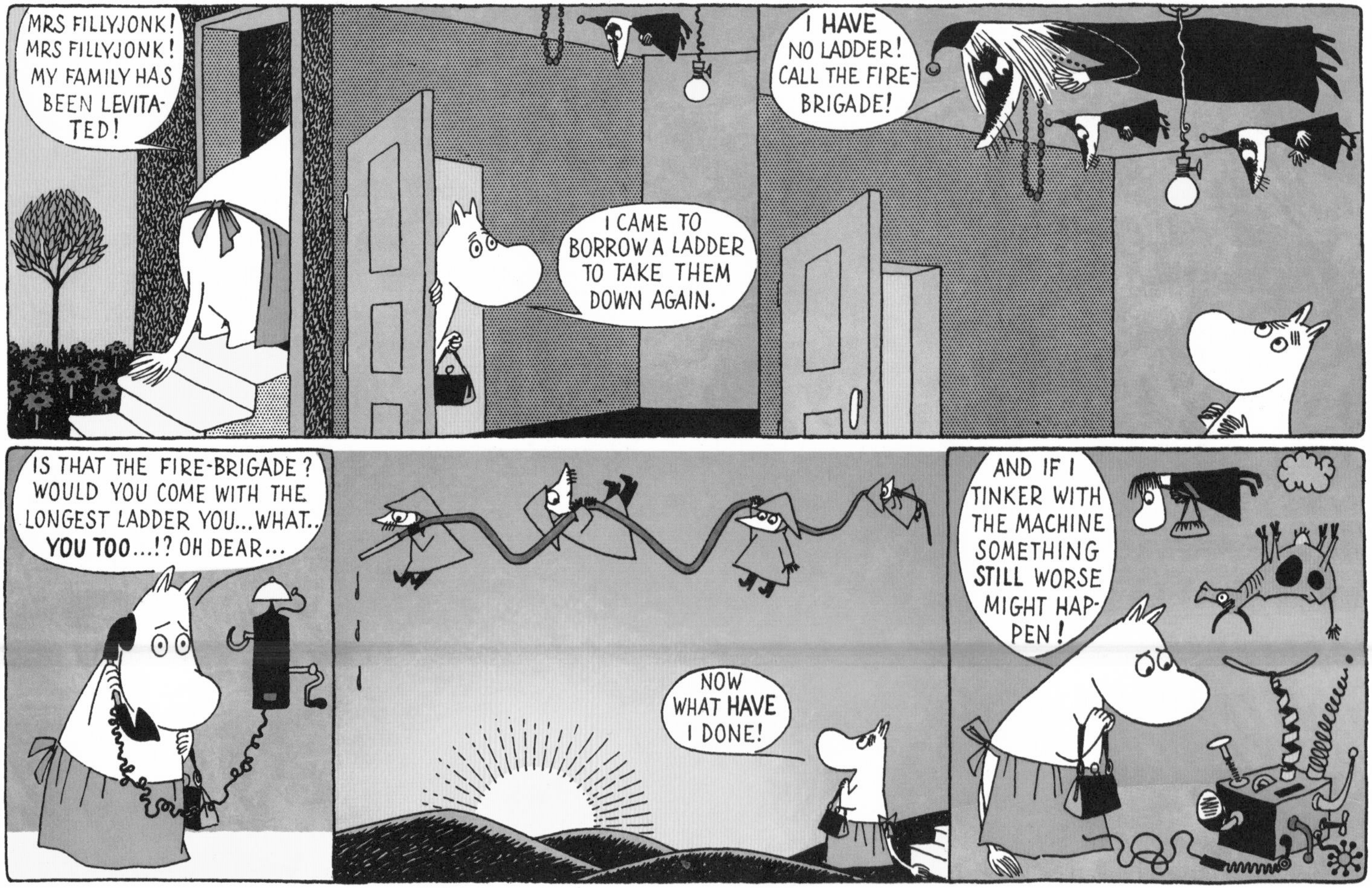
MRS FILLYJONK! MRS FILLYJONK! MY FAMILY HAS BEEN LEVITA-TED!
I CAME TO BORROW A LADDER TO TAKE THEM DOWN AGAIN.
I HAVE NO LADDER! CALL THE FIRE-BRIGADE!
IS THAT THE FIRE-BRIGADE? WOULD YOU COME WITH THE LONGEST LADDER YOU...WHAT.. YOU TOO...!? OH DEAR...
NOW WHAT HAVE I DONE!
AND IF I TINKER WITH THE MACHINE SOMETHING STILL WORSE MIGHT HAP-PEN!

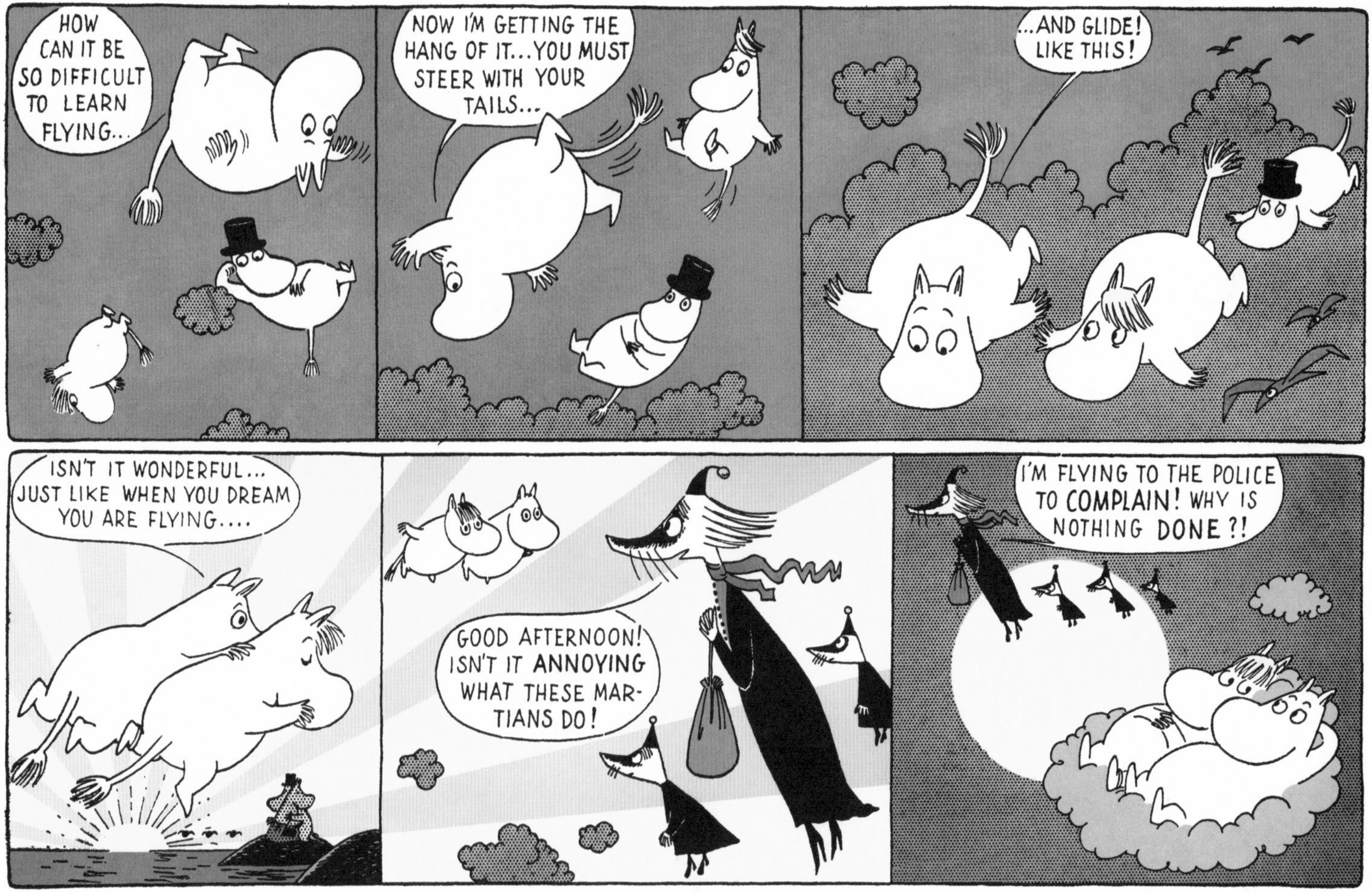
HOW CAN IT BE SO DIFFICULT TO LEARN FLYING..
NOW I'M GETTING THE HANG OF IT... YOU MUST STEER WITH YOUR TAILS...
...AND GLIDE! LIKE THIS!
ISN'T IT WONDERFUL... JUST LIKE WHEN YOU DREAM YOU ARE FLYING....
GOOD AFTERNOON! ISN'T IT ANNOYING WHAT THESE MAR-TIANS DO!
I'M FLYING TO THE POLICE TO COMPLAIN! WHY IS NOTHING DONE?!

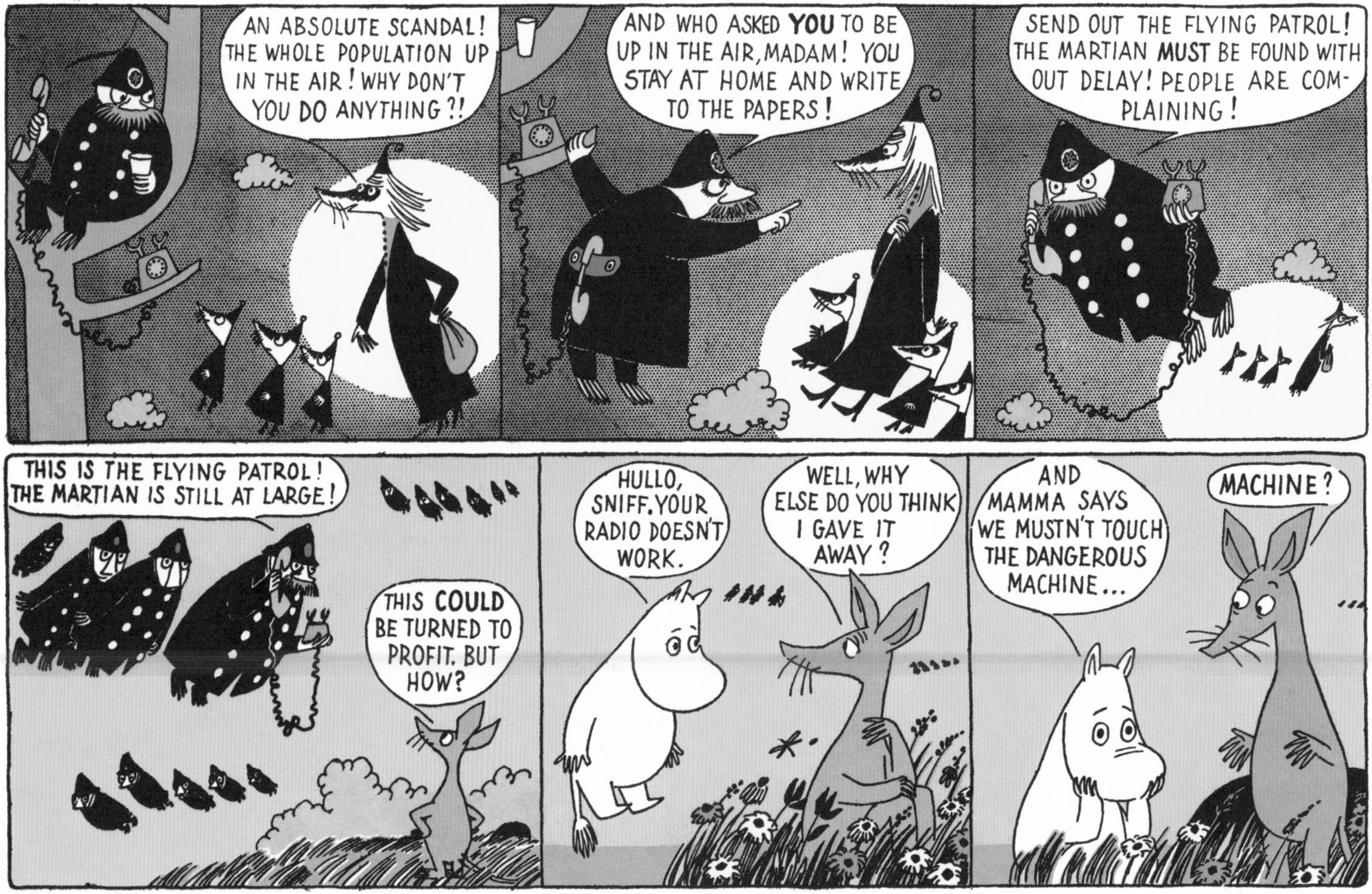
AN ABSOLUTE SCANDAL! THE WHOLE POPULATION UP IN THE AIR! WHY DON'T YOU DO ANYTHING?!
AND WHO ASKED YOU TO BE UP IN THE AIR, MADAM! YOU STAY AT HOME AND WRITE TO THE PAPERS!
SEND OUT THE FLYING PATROL! THE MARTIAN MUST BE FOUND WITH OUT DELAY! PEOPLE ARE COM-PLAINING!
THIS IS THE FLYING PATROL! THE MARTIAN IS STILL AT LARGE!
THIS COULD BE TURNED TO PROFIT. BUT HOW?
HULLO, SNIFF. YOUR RADIO DOESN'T WORK.
WELL, WHY ELSE DO YOU THINK I GAVE IT AWAY?
AND MAMMA SAYS WE MUSTN'T TOUCH THE DANGEROUS MACHINE...
MACHINE?

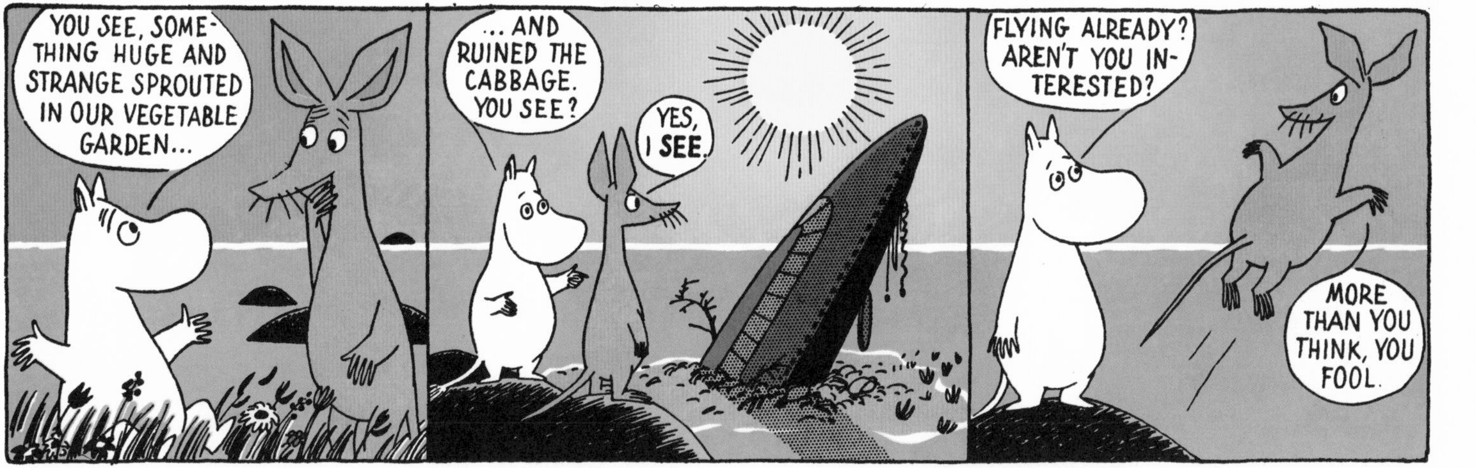
YOU SEE, SOMETHING HUGE AND STRANGE SPROUTED IN OUR VEGETABLE GARDEN...
...AND RUINED THE CABBAGE. YOU SEE?
YES, I **SEE**.
FLYING ALREADY? AREN'T YOU INTERESTED?
MORE THAN YOU THINK, YOU FOOL.

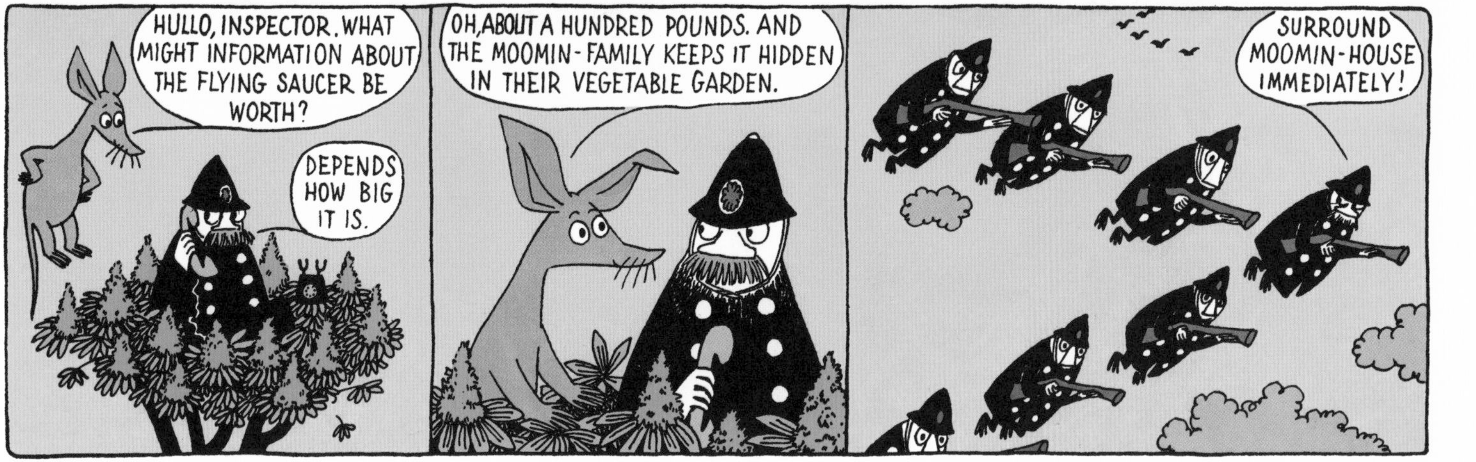
HULLO, INSPECTOR. WHAT MIGHT INFORMATION ABOUT THE FLYING SAUCER BE WORTH?
DEPENDS HOW BIG IT IS.
OH, ABOUT A HUNDRED POUNDS. AND THE MOOMIN-FAMILY KEEPS IT HIDDEN IN THEIR VEGETABLE GARDEN.
SURROUND MOOMIN-HOUSE IMMEDIATELY!

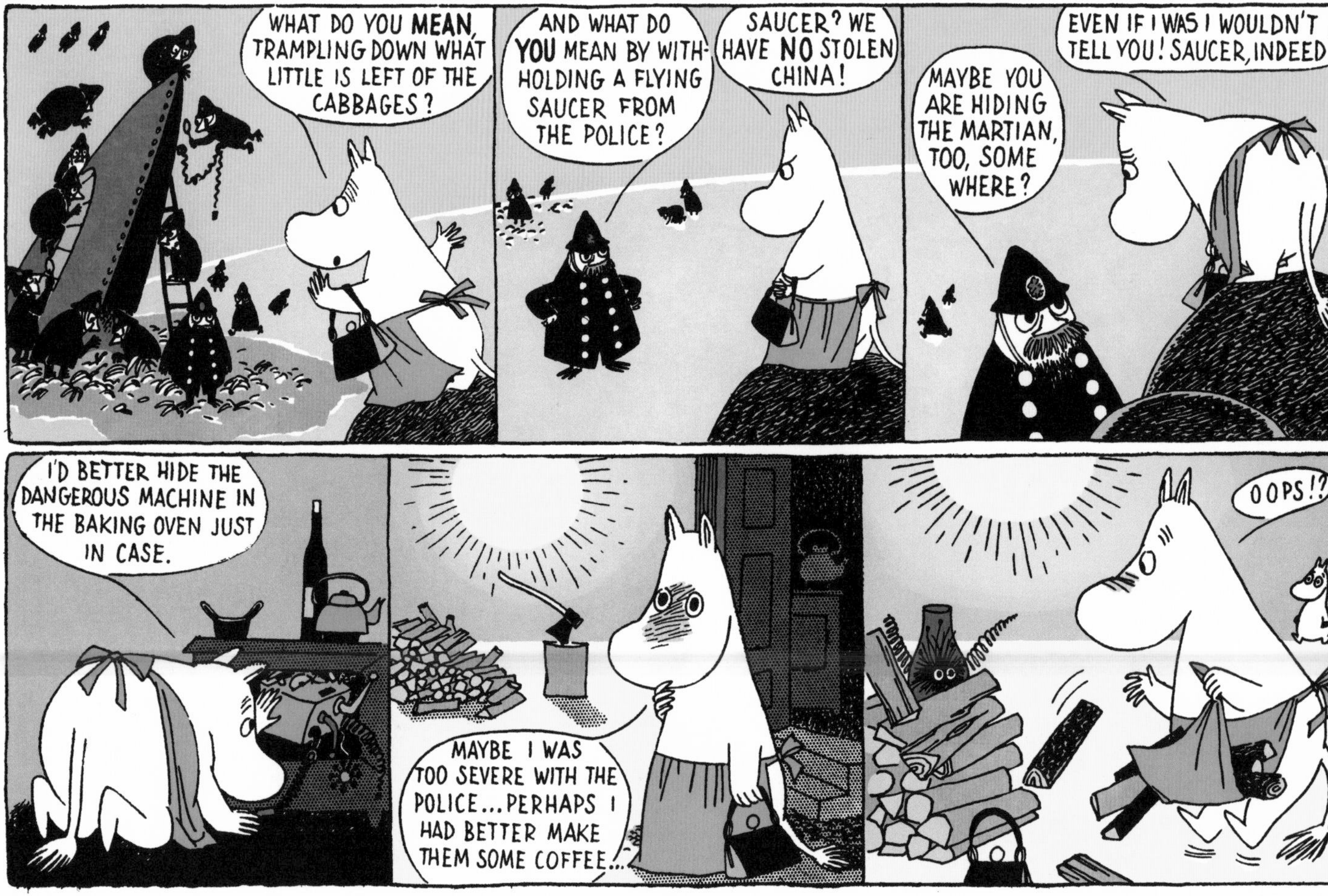
WHAT DO YOU MEAN, TRAMPLING DOWN WHAT LITTLE IS LEFT OF THE CABBAGES?
AND WHAT DO YOU MEAN BY WITH-HOLDING A FLYING SAUCER FROM THE POLICE?
SAUCER? WE HAVE NO STOLEN CHINA!
MAYBE YOU ARE HIDING THE MARTIAN, TOO, SOME WHERE?
EVEN IF I WAS I WOULDN'T TELL YOU! SAUCER, INDEED!
I'D BETTER HIDE THE DANGEROUS MACHINE IN THE BAKING OVEN JUST IN CASE.
MAYBE I WAS TOO SEVERE WITH THE POLICE... PERHAPS I HAD BETTER MAKE THEM SOME COFFEE...
OOPS!?

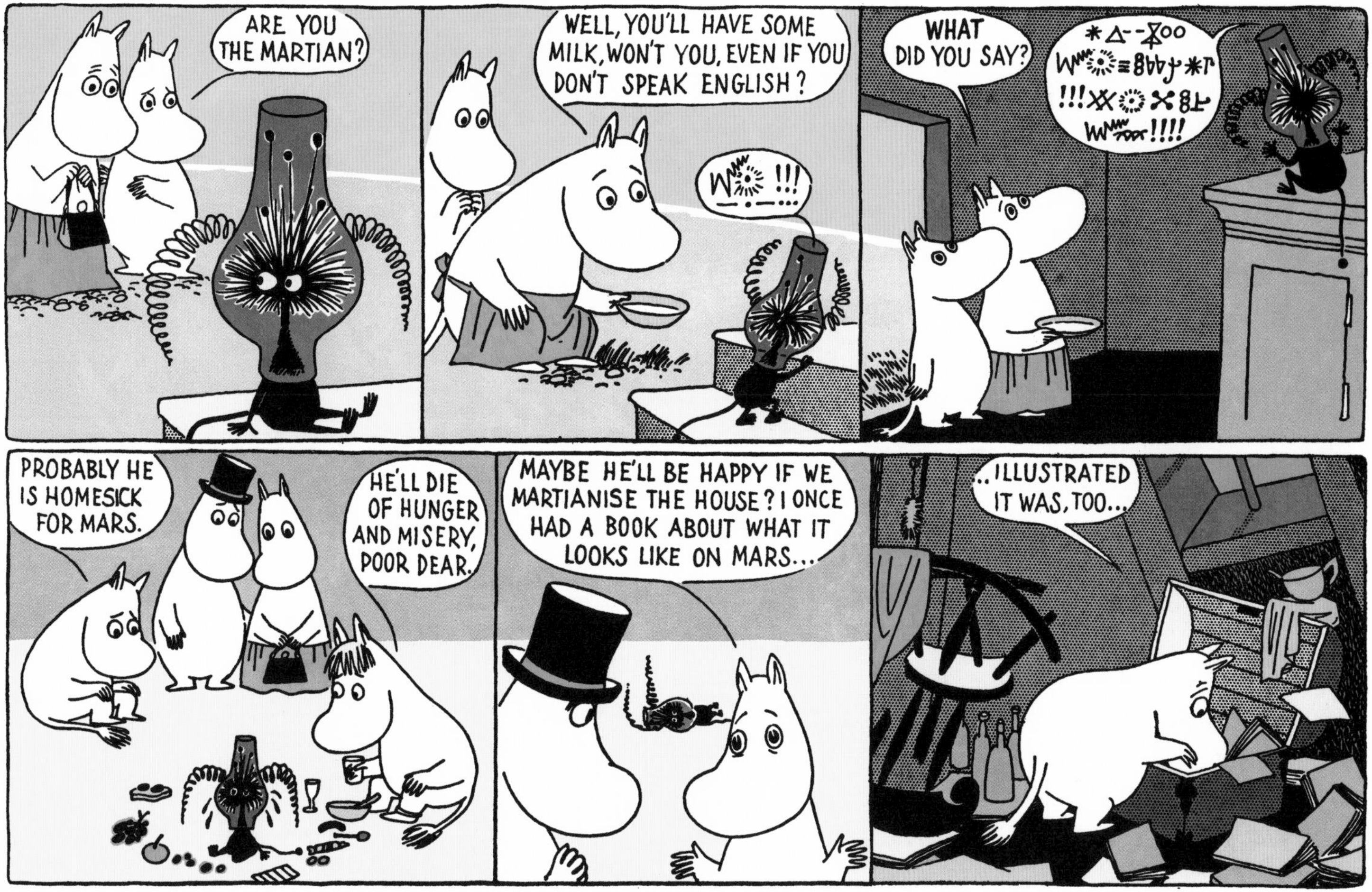
ARE YOU THE MARTIAN?
WELL, YOU'LL HAVE SOME MILK, WON'T YOU, EVEN IF YOU DON'T SPEAK ENGLISH?
WHAT DID YOU SAY?
PROBABLY HE IS HOMESICK FOR MARS.
HE'LL DIE OF HUNGER AND MISERY, POOR DEAR.
MAYBE HE'LL BE HAPPY IF WE MARTIANISE THE HOUSE? I ONCE HAD A BOOK ABOUT WHAT IT LOOKS LIKE ON MARS...
...ILLUSTRATED IT WAS, TOO...

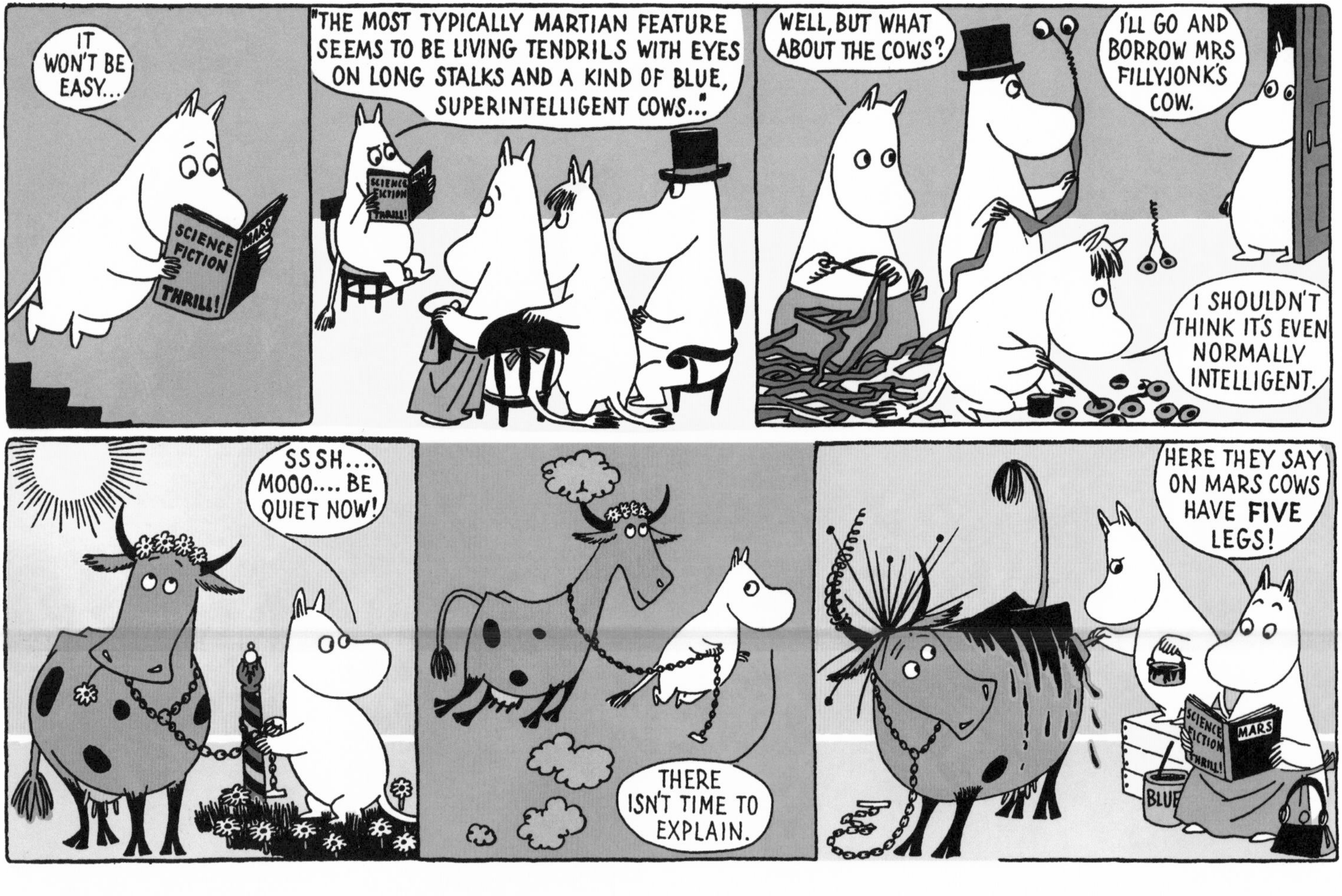
IT WON'T BE EASY...
"THE MOST TYPICALLY MARTIAN FEATURE SEEMS TO BE LIVING TENDRILS WITH EYES ON LONG STALKS AND A KIND OF BLUE, SUPERINTELLIGENT COWS..."
SCIENCE FICTION THRILL!
MARS
WELL, BUT WHAT ABOUT THE COWS?
I'LL GO AND BORROW MRS FILLYJONK'S COW.
I SHOULDN'T THINK IT'S EVEN NORMALLY INTELLIGENT.
SSSH.... MOOO.... BE QUIET NOW!
THERE ISN'T TIME TO EXPLAIN.
HERE THEY SAY ON MARS COWS HAVE **FIVE** LEGS!
BLUE

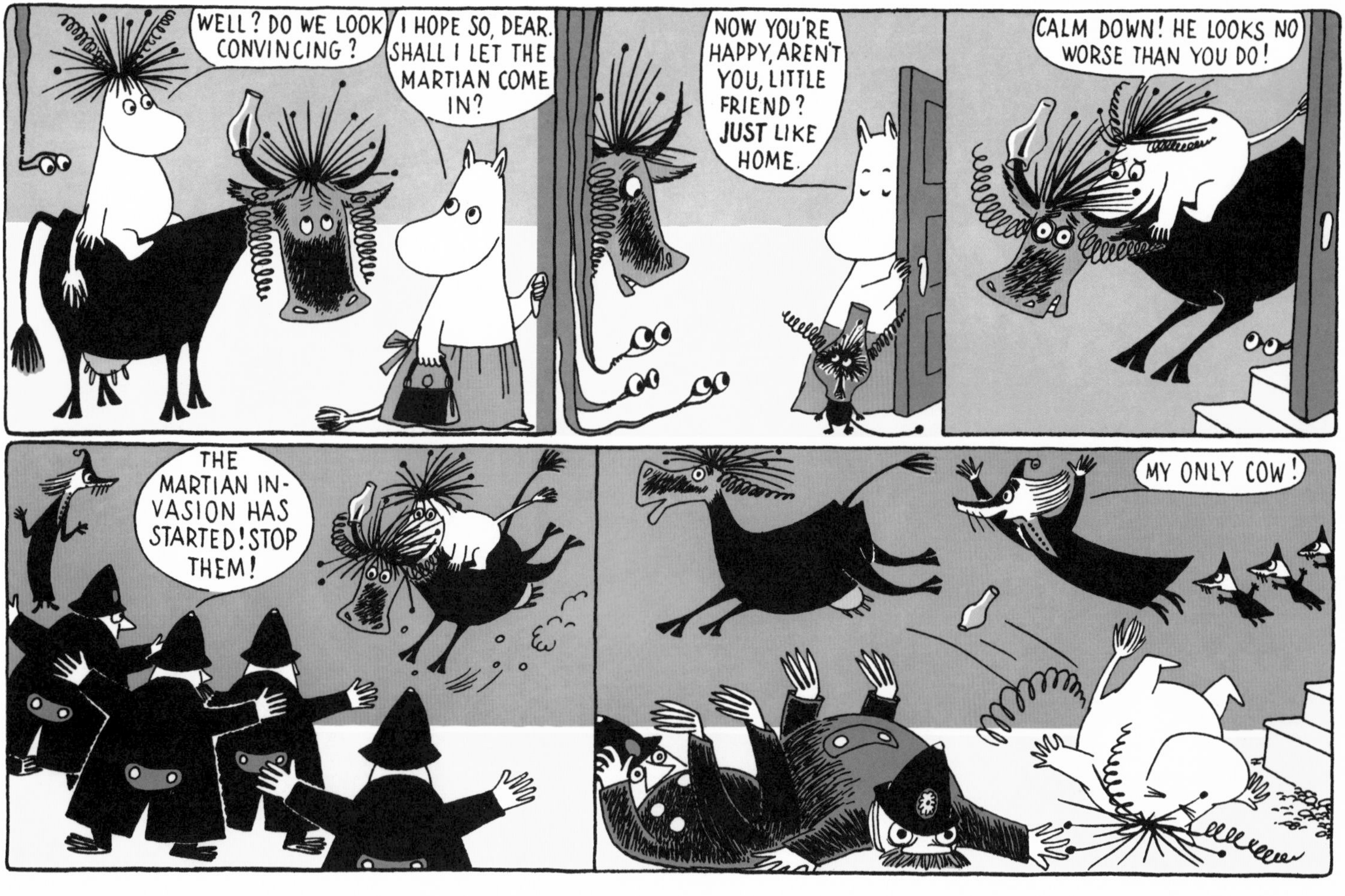
WELL? DO WE LOOK CONVINCING?
I HOPE SO, DEAR. SHALL I LET THE MARTIAN COME IN?
NOW YOU'RE HAPPY, AREN'T YOU, LITTLE FRIEND? JUST LIKE HOME.
CALM DOWN! HE LOOKS NO WORSE THAN YOU DO!
THE MARTIAN INVASION HAS STARTED! STOP THEM!
MY ONLY COW!

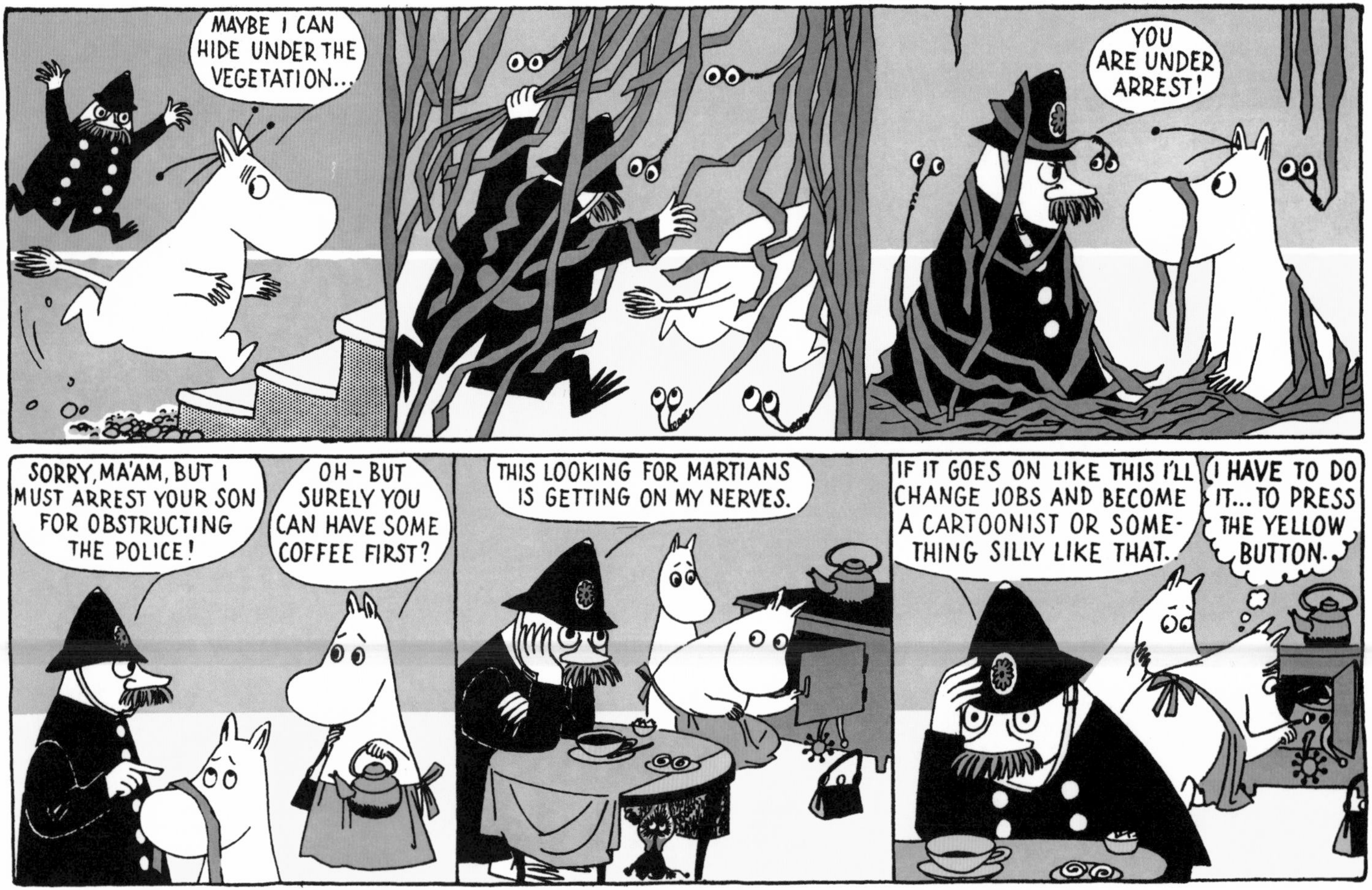
MAYBE I CAN HIDE UNDER THE VEGETATION...
YOU ARE UNDER ARREST!
SORRY, MA'AM, BUT I MUST ARREST YOUR SON FOR OBSTRUCTING THE POLICE!
OH - BUT SURELY YOU CAN HAVE SOME COFFEE FIRST?
THIS LOOKING FOR MARTIANS IS GETTING ON MY NERVES.
IF IT GOES ON LIKE THIS I'LL CHANGE JOBS AND BECOME A CARTOONIST OR SOMETHING SILLY LIKE THAT..
I HAVE TO DO IT... TO PRESS THE YELLOW BUTTON.

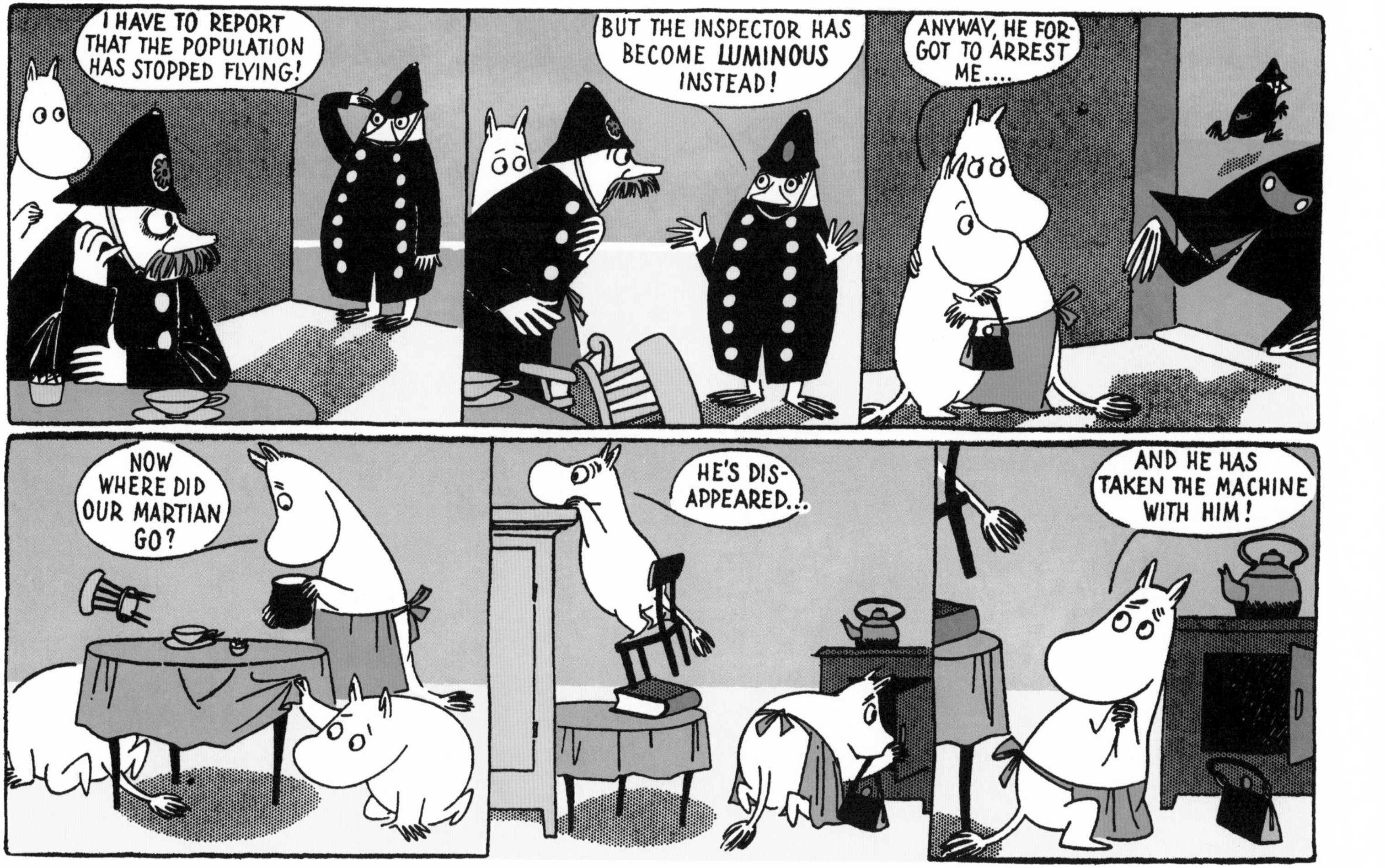
I HAVE TO REPORT THAT THE POPULATION HAS STOPPED FLYING!
BUT THE INSPECTOR HAS BECOME LUMINOUS INSTEAD!
ANYWAY, HE FORGOT TO ARREST ME....
NOW WHERE DID OUR MARTIAN GO?
HE'S DISAPPEARED...
AND HE HAS TAKEN THE MACHINE WITH HIM!

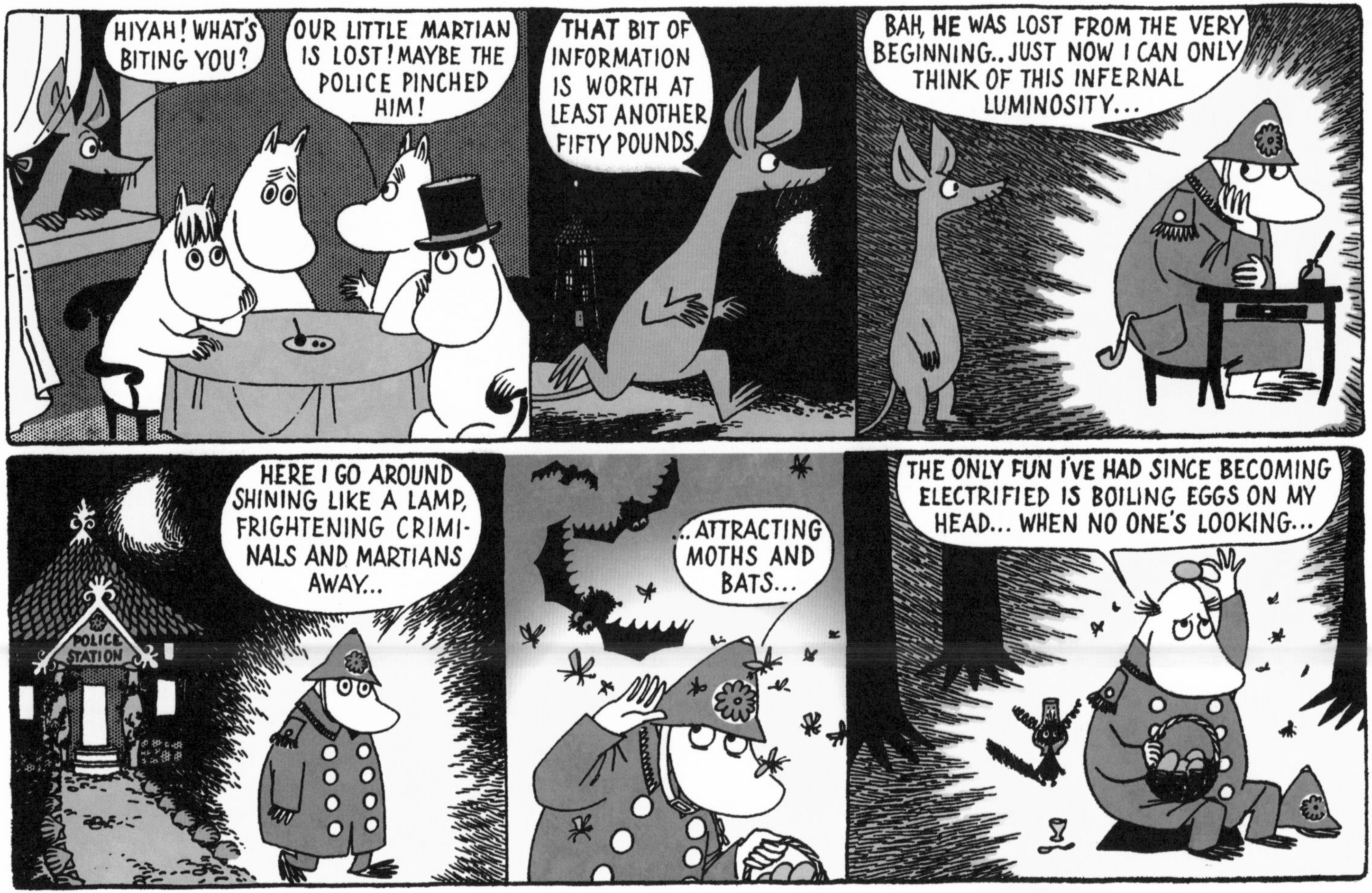
HIYAH! WHAT'S BITING YOU?
OUR LITTLE MARTIAN IS LOST! MAYBE THE POLICE PINCHED HIM!
THAT BIT OF INFORMATION IS WORTH AT LEAST ANOTHER FIFTY POUNDS.
BAH, HE WAS LOST FROM THE VERY BEGINNING.. JUST NOW I CAN ONLY THINK OF THIS INFERNAL LUMINOSITY...
HERE I GO AROUND SHINING LIKE A LAMP, FRIGHTENING CRIMINALS AND MARTIANS AWAY...
POLICE STATION
...ATTRACTING MOTHS AND BATS...
THE ONLY FUN I'VE HAD SINCE BECOMING ELECTRIFIED IS BOILING EGGS ON MY HEAD... WHEN NO ONE'S LOOKING...

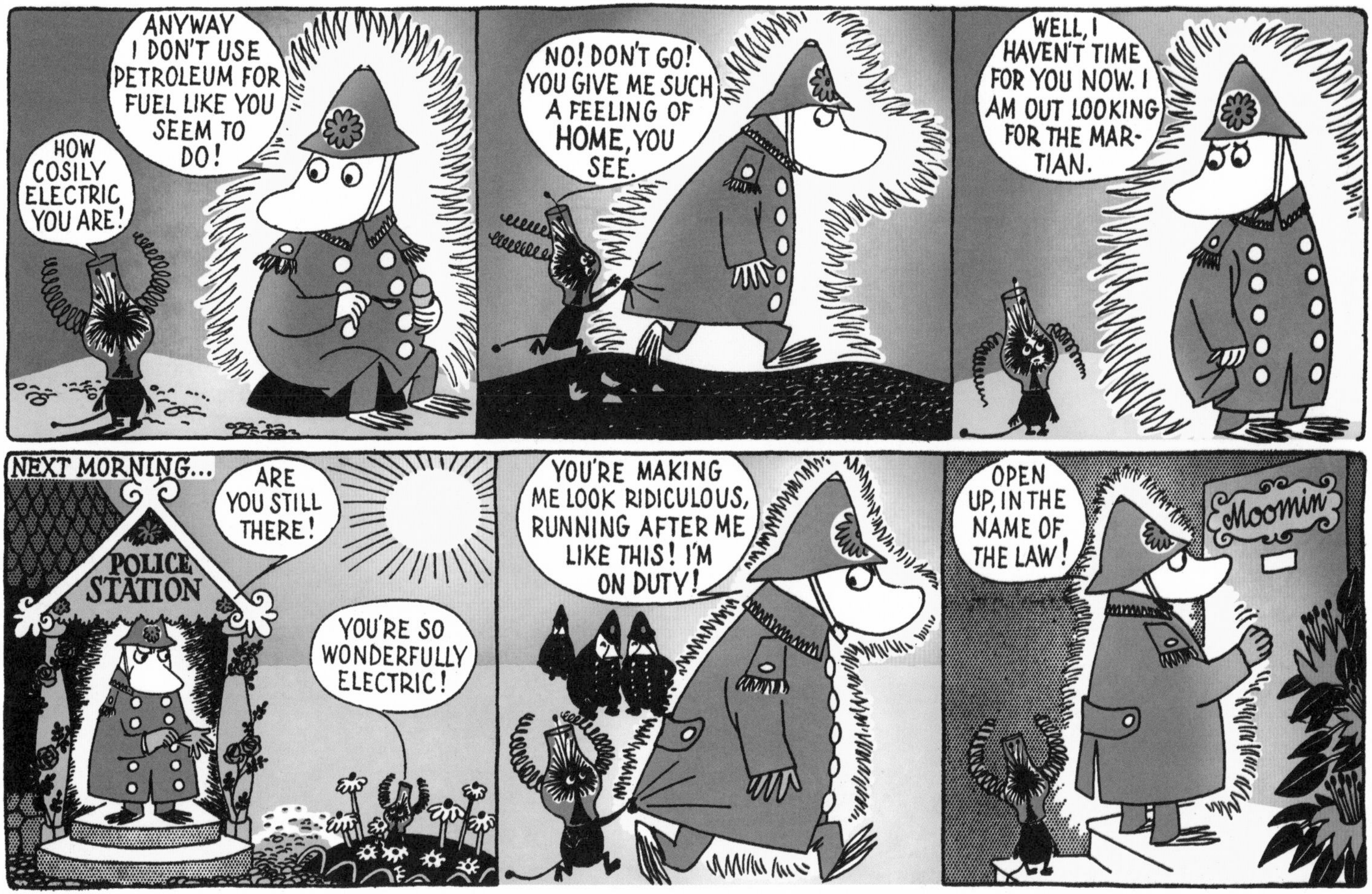
HOW COSILY ELECTRIC YOU ARE!
ANYWAY I DON'T USE PETROLEUM FOR FUEL LIKE YOU SEEM TO DO!
NO! DON'T GO! YOU GIVE ME SUCH A FEELING OF HOME, YOU SEE.
WELL, I HAVEN'T TIME FOR YOU NOW. I AM OUT LOOKING FOR THE MAR-TIAN.
NEXT MORNING...
POLICE STATION
ARE YOU STILL THERE!
YOU'RE SO WONDERFULLY ELECTRIC!
YOU'RE MAKING ME LOOK RIDICULOUS, RUNNING AFTER ME LIKE THIS! I'M ON DUTY!
OPEN UP, IN THE NAME OF THE LAW!
Moomin

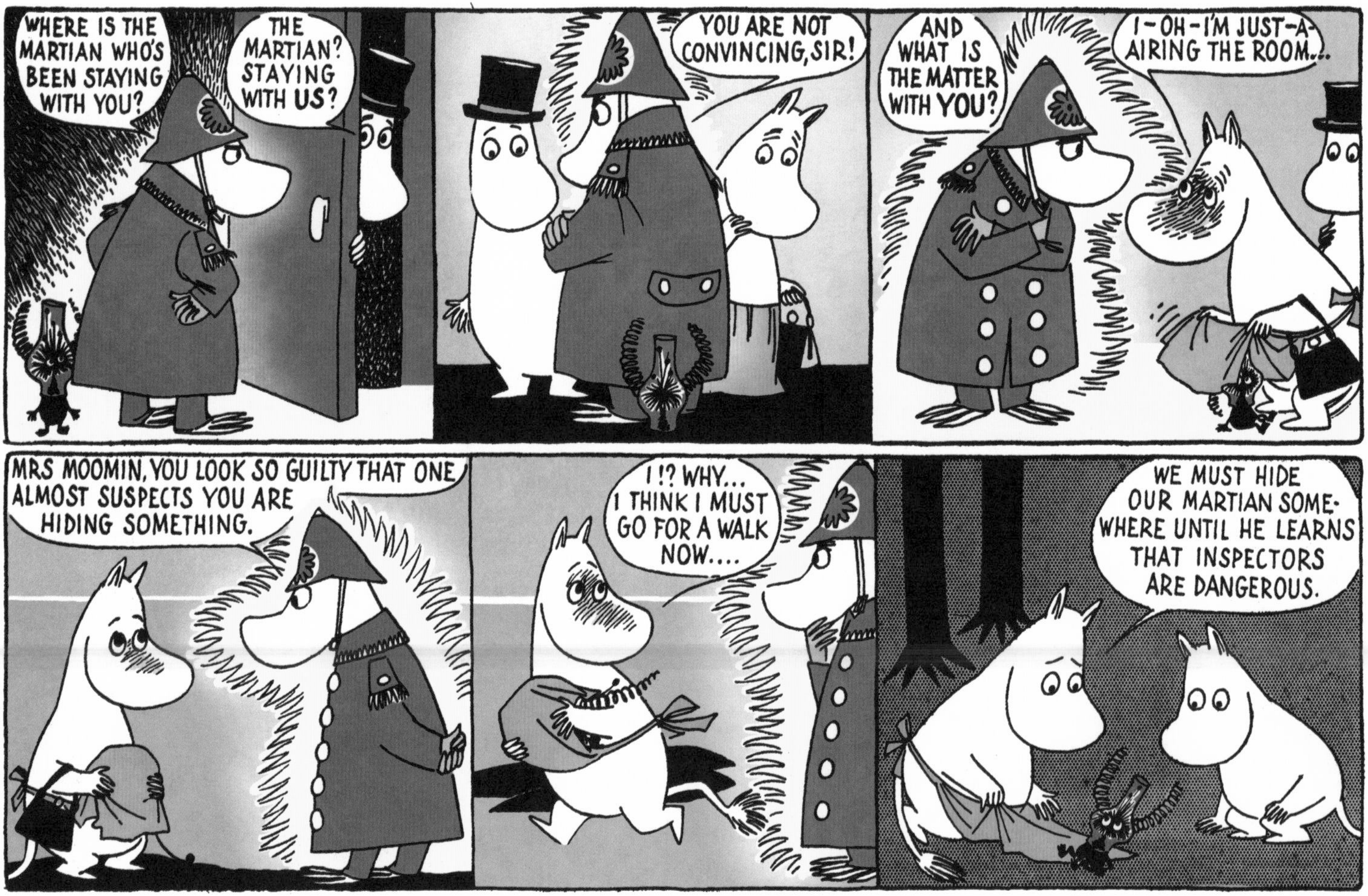
WHERE IS THE MARTIAN WHO'S BEEN STAYING WITH YOU?
THE MARTIAN? STAYING WITH US?
YOU ARE NOT CONVINCING, SIR!
AND WHAT IS THE MATTER WITH YOU?
I-OH-I'M JUST-A-AIRING THE ROOM...
MRS MOOMIN, YOU LOOK SO GUILTY THAT ONE ALMOST SUSPECTS YOU ARE HIDING SOMETHING.
I!? WHY... I THINK I MUST GO FOR A WALK NOW....
WE MUST HIDE OUR MARTIAN SOMEWHERE UNTIL HE LEARNS THAT INSPECTORS ARE DANGEROUS.

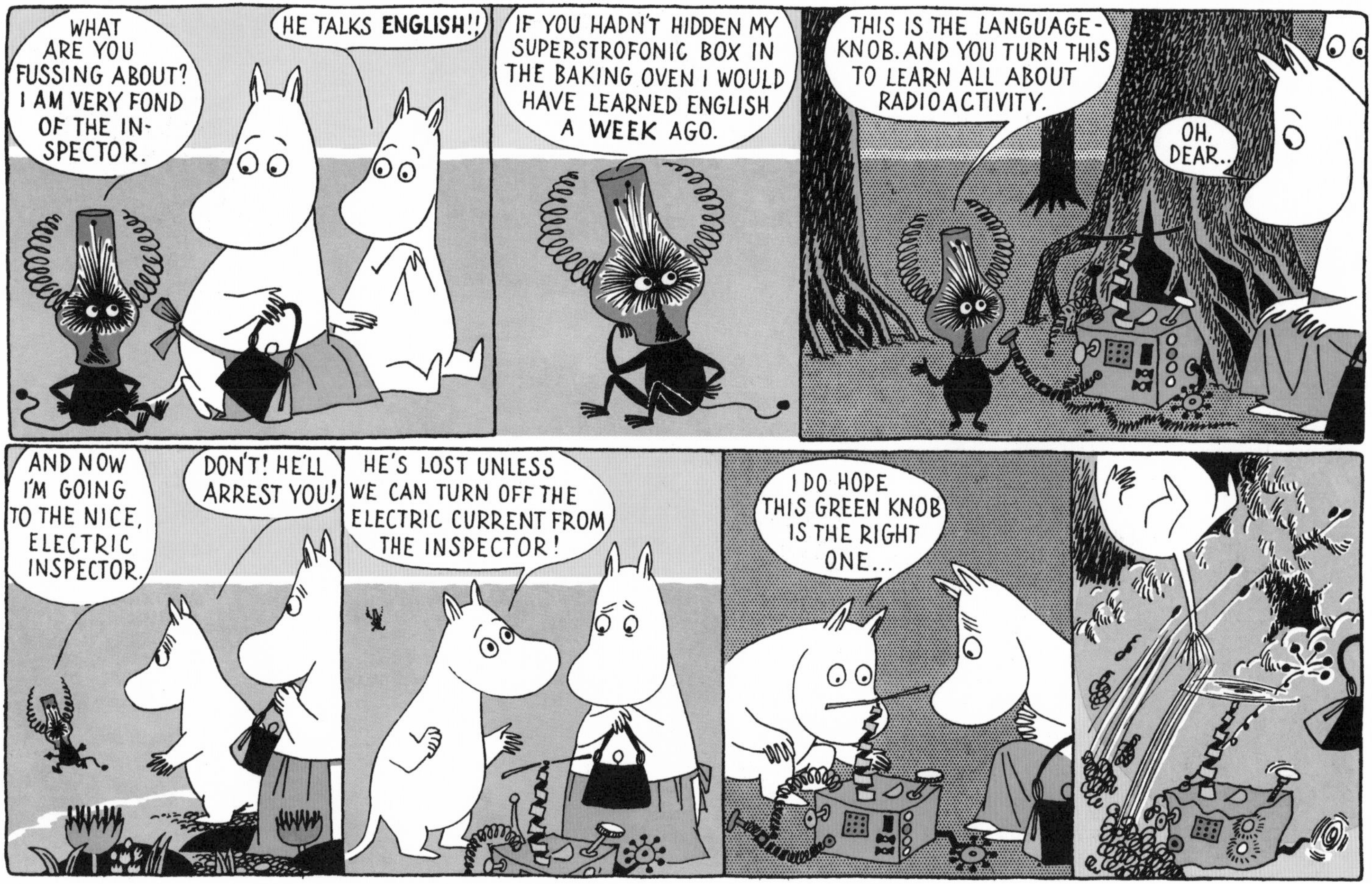
WHAT ARE YOU FUSSING ABOUT? I AM VERY FOND OF THE IN-SPECTOR.
HE TALKS ENGLISH!!
IF YOU HADN'T HIDDEN MY SUPERSTROFONIC BOX IN THE BAKING OVEN I WOULD HAVE LEARNED ENGLISH A WEEK AGO.
THIS IS THE LANGUAGE-KNOB. AND YOU TURN THIS TO LEARN ALL ABOUT RADIOACTIVITY.
OH, DEAR..
AND NOW I'M GOING TO THE NICE, ELECTRIC INSPECTOR.
DON'T! HE'LL ARREST YOU!
HE'S LOST UNLESS WE CAN TURN OFF THE ELECTRIC CURRENT FROM THE INSPECTOR!
I DO HOPE THIS GREEN KNOB IS THE RIGHT ONE...

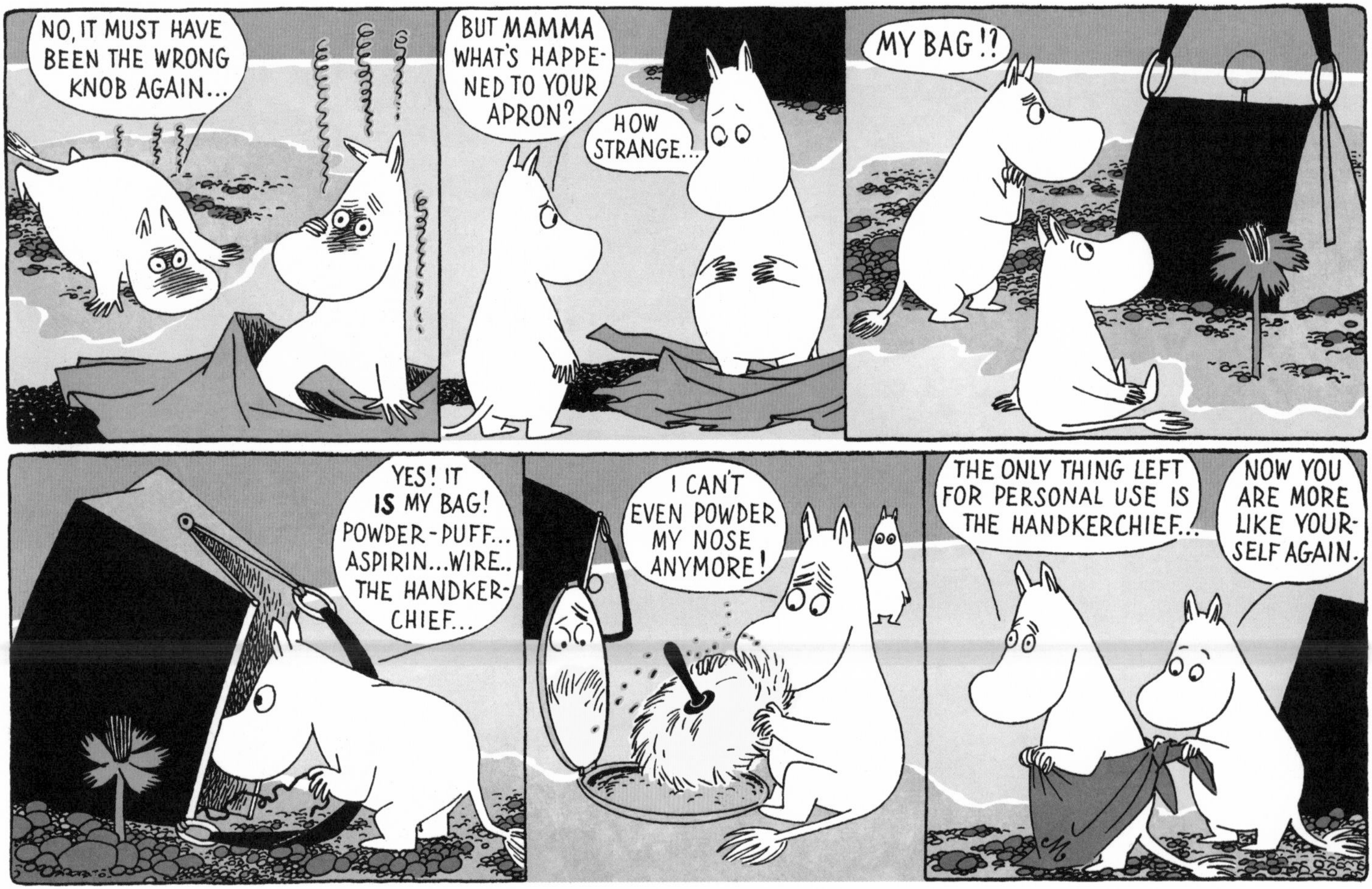
NO, IT MUST HAVE BEEN THE WRONG KNOB AGAIN...
BUT MAMMA WHAT'S HAPPE-NED TO YOUR APRON?
HOW STRANGE...
MY BAG!?
YES! IT **IS** MY BAG! POWDER-PUFF... ASPIRIN...WIRE.. THE HANDKER-CHIEF...
I CAN'T EVEN POWDER MY NOSE ANYMORE!
THE ONLY THING LEFT FOR PERSONAL USE IS THE HANDKERCHIEF...
NOW YOU ARE MORE LIKE YOUR-SELF AGAIN.

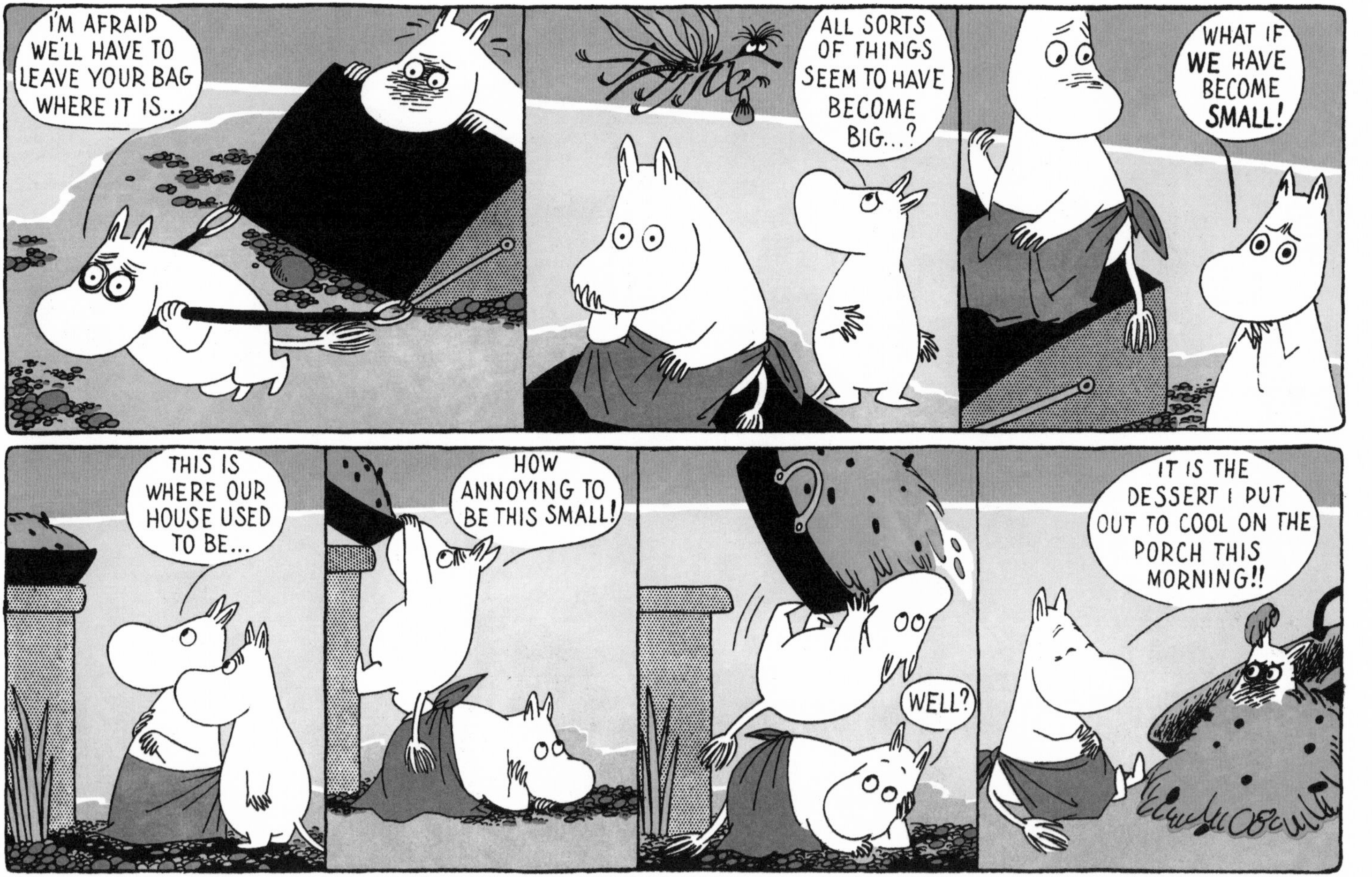
I'M AFRAID WE'LL HAVE TO LEAVE YOUR BAG WHERE IT IS...
ALL SORTS OF THINGS SEEM TO HAVE BECOME BIG...?
WHAT IF **WE** HAVE BECOME **SMALL**!
THIS IS WHERE OUR HOUSE USED TO BE...
HOW ANNOYING TO BE THIS SMALL!
WELL?
IT IS THE DESSERT I PUT OUT TO COOL ON THE PORCH THIS MORNING!!

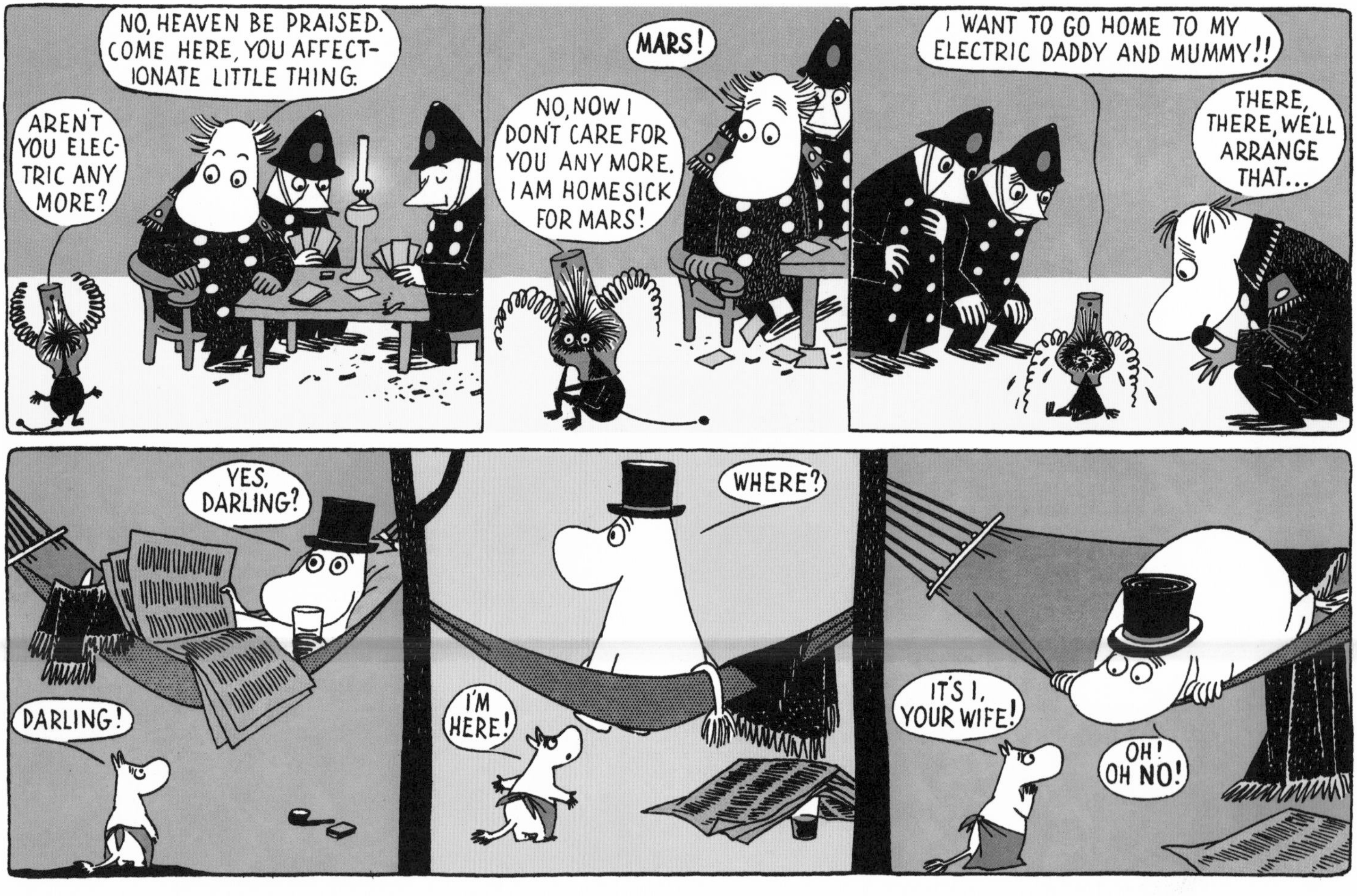
ARE'NT YOU ELECTRIC ANY MORE?
NO, HEAVEN BE PRAISED. COME HERE, YOU AFFECTIONATE LITTLE THING.
NO, NOW I DON'T CARE FOR YOU ANY MORE. I AM HOMESICK FOR MARS!
MARS!
I WANT TO GO HOME TO MY ELECTRIC DADDY AND MUMMY!!
THERE, THERE, WE'LL ARRANGE THAT...
DARLING!
YES, DARLING?
I'M HERE!
WHERE?
IT'S I, YOUR WIFE!
OH! OH NO!

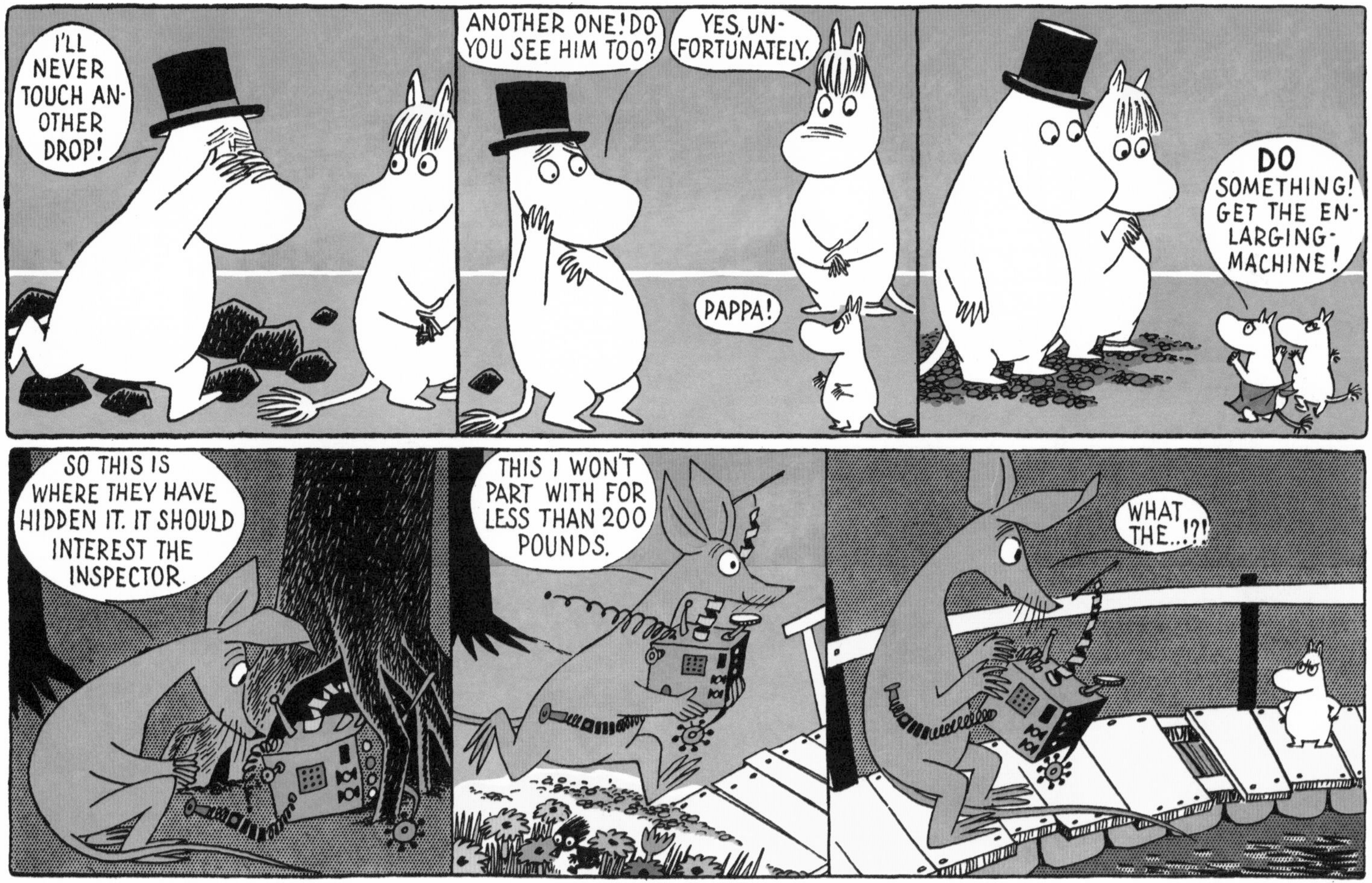
I'LL NEVER TOUCH ANOTHER DROP!
ANOTHER ONE! DO YOU SEE HIM TOO?
YES, UNFORTUNATELY.
PAPPA!
DO SOMETHING! GET THE ENLARGING-MACHINE!
SO THIS IS WHERE THEY HAVE HIDDEN IT. IT SHOULD INTEREST THE INSPECTOR.
THIS I WON'T PART WITH FOR LESS THAN 200 POUNDS.
WHAT THE...!?!

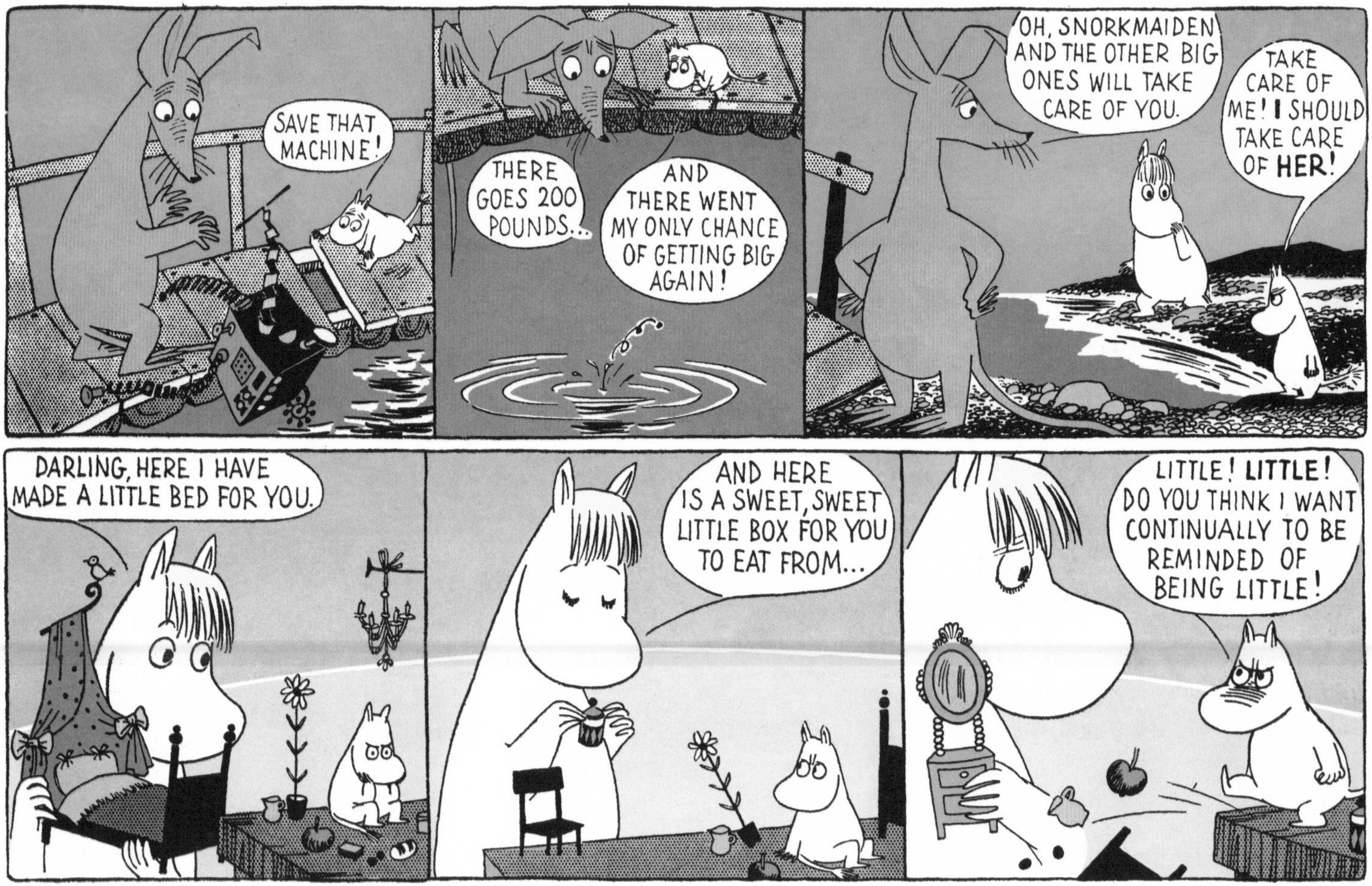
SAVE THAT MACHINE!
THERE GOES 200 POUNDS...
AND THERE WENT MY ONLY CHANCE OF GETTING BIG AGAIN!
OH, SNORKMAIDEN AND THE OTHER BIG ONES WILL TAKE CARE OF YOU.
TAKE CARE OF ME! I SHOULD TAKE CARE OF **HER**!
DARLING, HERE I HAVE MADE A LITTLE BED FOR YOU.
AND HERE IS A SWEET, SWEET LITTLE BOX FOR YOU TO EAT FROM...
LITTLE! **LITTLE!** DO YOU THINK I WANT CONTINUALLY TO BE REMINDED OF BEING LITTLE!

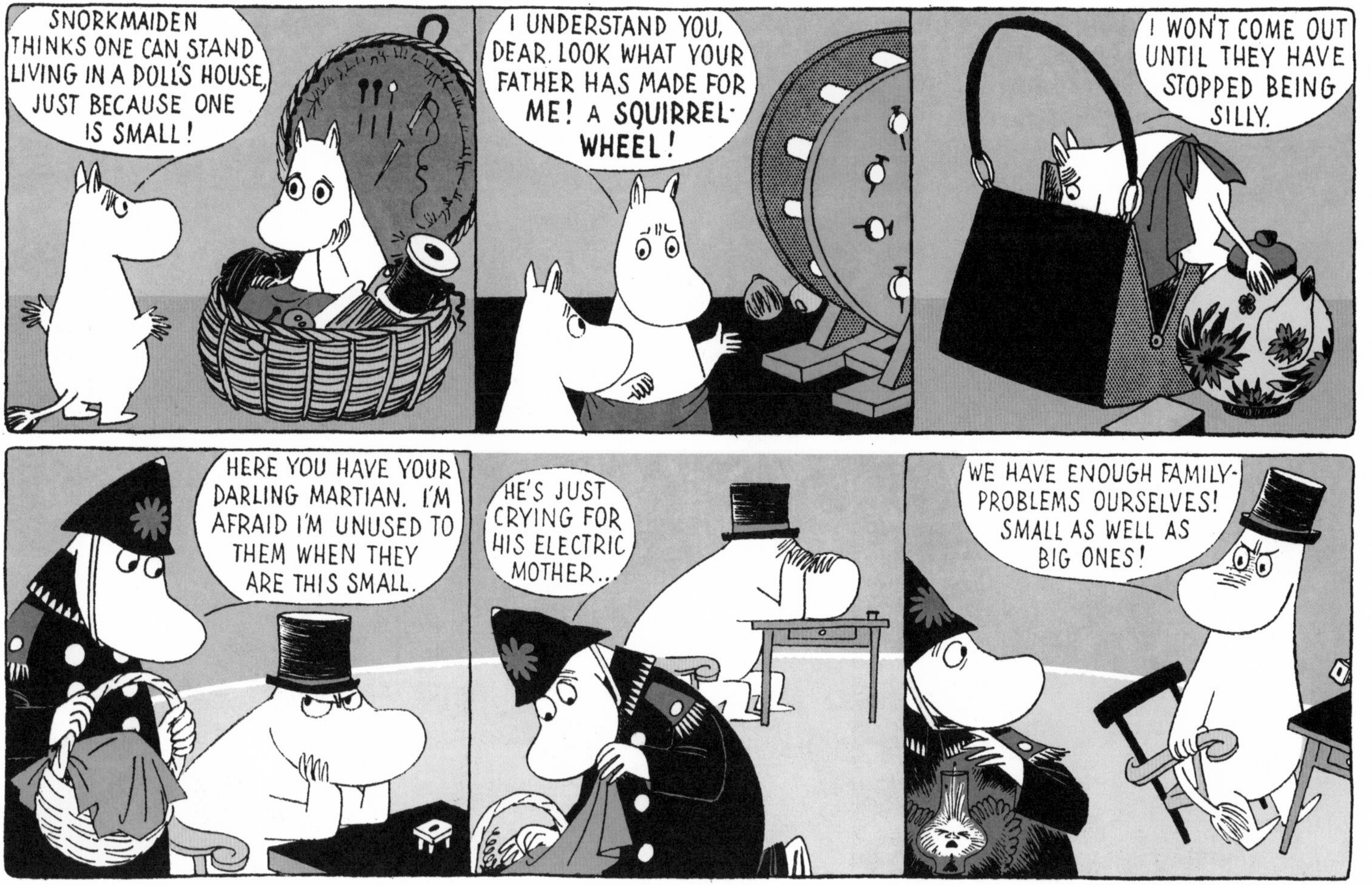
SNORKMAIDEN THINKS ONE CAN STAND LIVING IN A DOLL'S HOUSE, JUST BECAUSE ONE IS SMALL!
I UNDERSTAND YOU, DEAR. LOOK WHAT YOUR FATHER HAS MADE FOR ME! A SQUIRREL-WHEEL!
I WON'T COME OUT UNTIL THEY HAVE STOPPED BEING SILLY.
HERE YOU HAVE YOUR DARLING MARTIAN. I'M AFRAID I'M UNUSED TO THEM WHEN THEY ARE THIS SMALL.
HE'S JUST CRYING FOR HIS ELECTRIC MOTHER...
WE HAVE ENOUGH FAMILY-PROBLEMS OURSELVES! SMALL AS WELL AS BIG ONES!

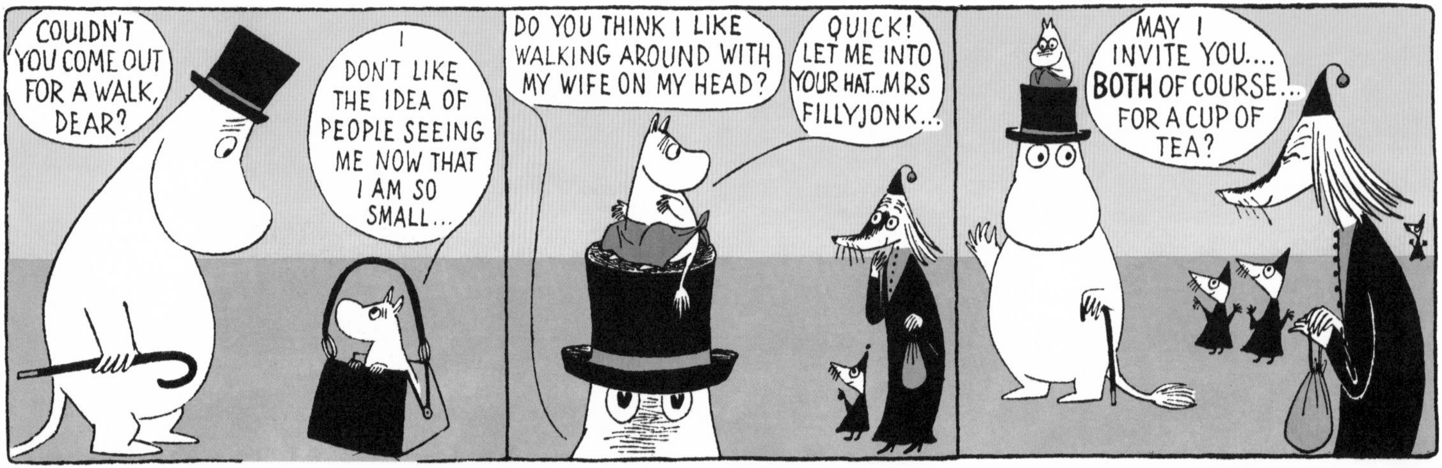
COULDN'T YOU COME OUT FOR A WALK, DEAR?
I DON'T LIKE THE IDEA OF PEOPLE SEEING ME NOW THAT I AM SO SMALL...
DO YOU THINK I LIKE WALKING AROUND WITH MY WIFE ON MY HEAD?
QUICK! LET ME INTO YOUR HAT...MRS FILLYJONK...
MAY I INVITE YOU.... **BOTH** OF COURSE... FOR A CUP OF TEA?

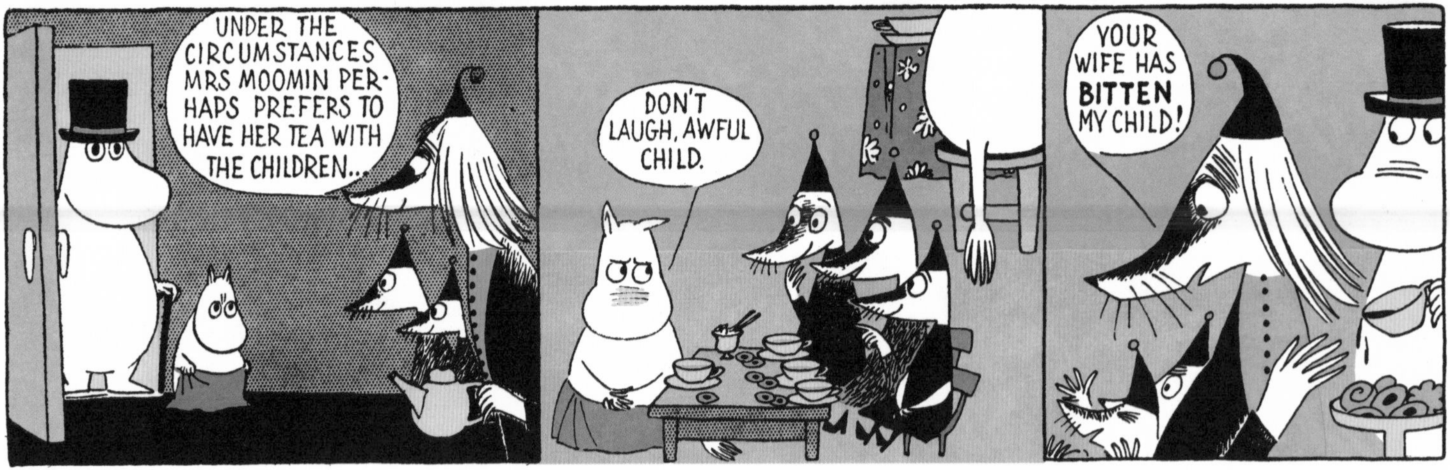
UNDER THE CIRCUMSTANCES MRS MOOMIN PER-HAPS PREFERS TO HAVE HER TEA WITH THE CHILDREN...
DON'T LAUGH, AWFUL CHILD.
YOUR WIFE HAS **BITTEN** MY CHILD!

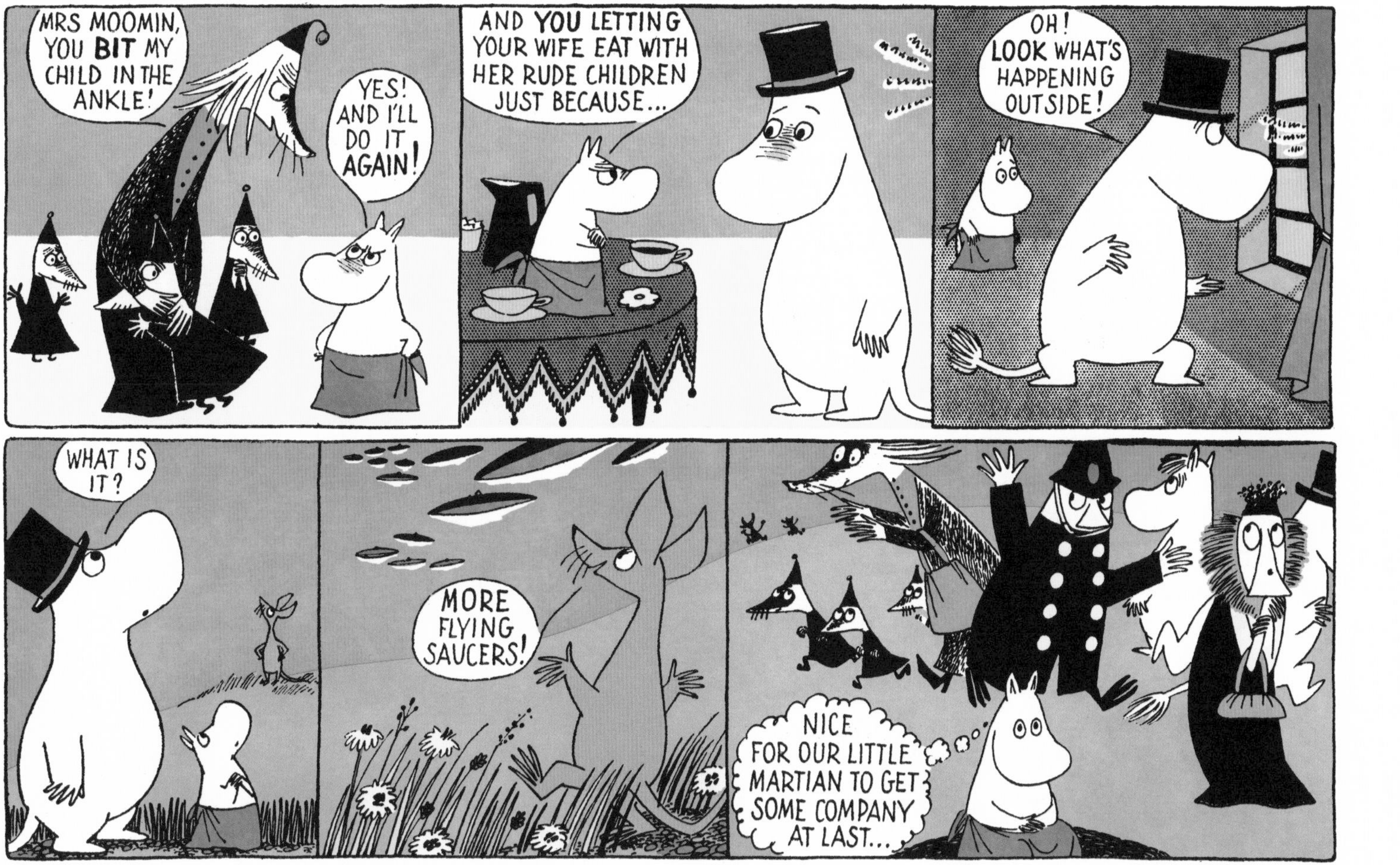
MRS MOOMIN, YOU BIT MY CHILD IN THE ANKLE!
YES! AND I'LL DO IT AGAIN!
AND YOU LETTING YOUR WIFE EAT WITH HER RUDE CHILDREN JUST BECAUSE...
OH! LOOK WHAT'S HAPPENING OUTSIDE!
WHAT IS IT?
MORE FLYING SAUCERS!
NICE FOR OUR LITTLE MARTIAN TO GET SOME COMPANY AT LAST...

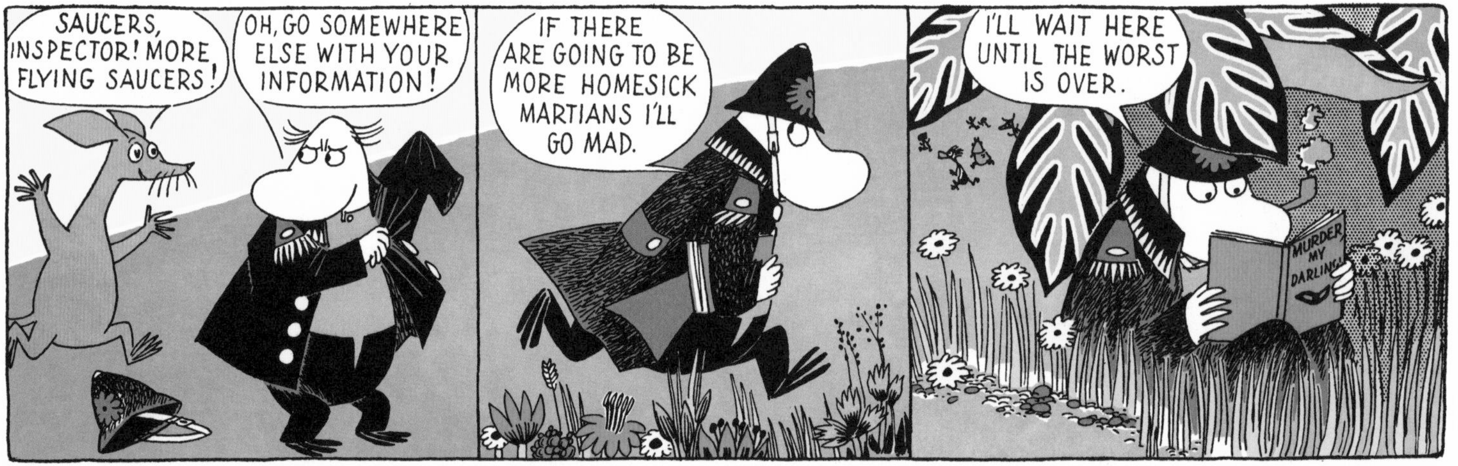
SAUCERS, INSPECTOR! MORE FLYING SAUCERS!
OH, GO SOMEWHERE ELSE WITH YOUR INFORMATION!
IF THERE ARE GOING TO BE MORE HOMESICK MARTIANS I'LL GO MAD.
I'LL WAIT HERE UNTIL THE WORST IS OVER.
MURDER MY DARLING

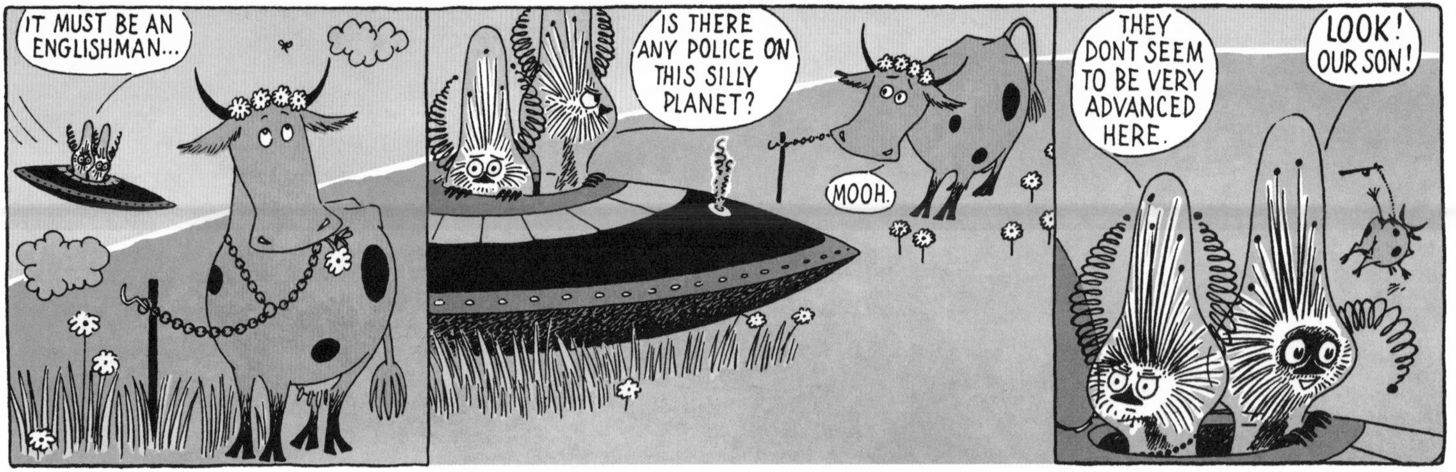
IT MUST BE AN ENGLISHMAN...
IS THERE ANY POLICE ON THIS SILLY PLANET?
MOOH.
THEY DON'T SEEM TO BE VERY ADVANCED HERE.
LOOK! OUR SON!

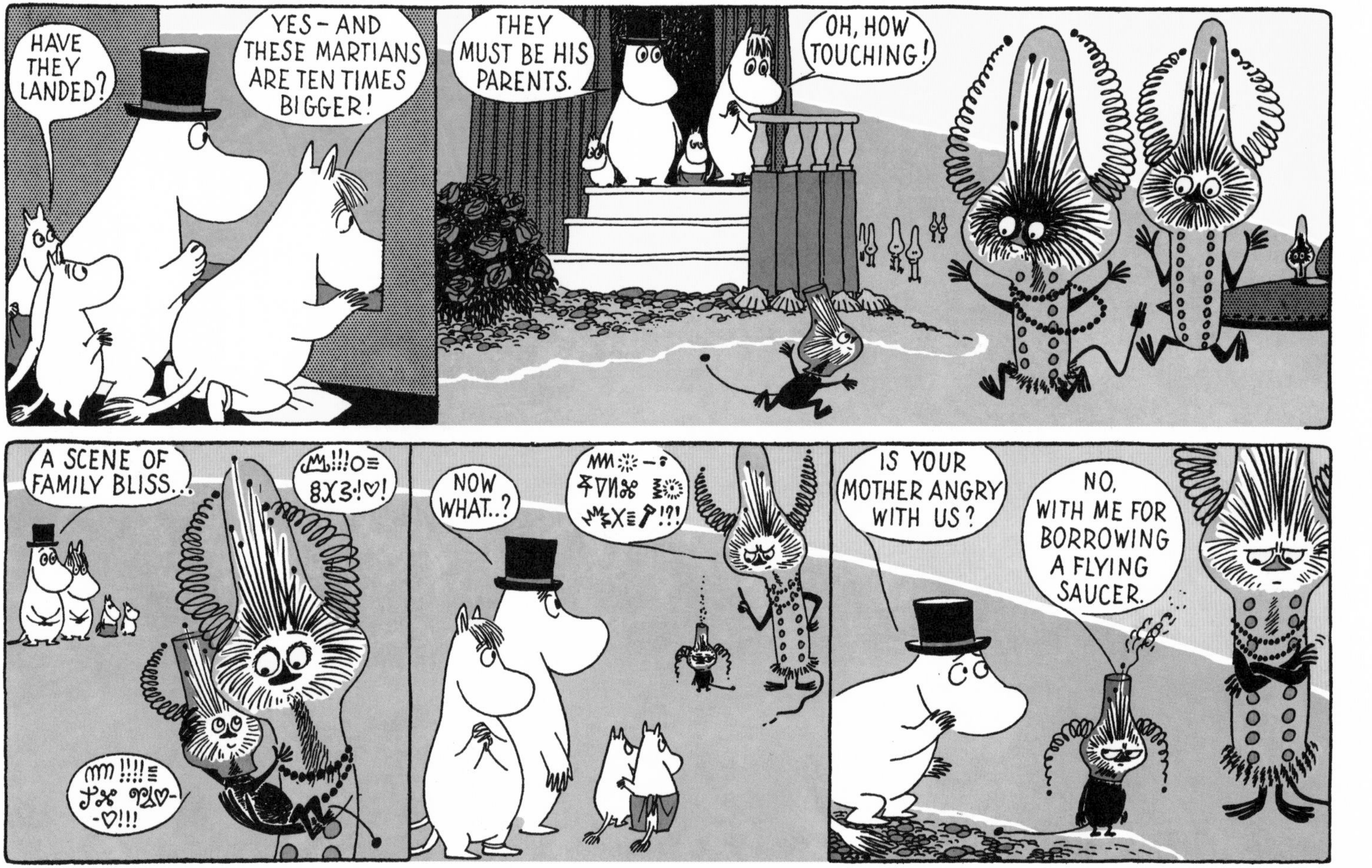
HAVE THEY LANDED?
YES – AND THESE MARTIANS ARE TEN TIMES BIGGER!
THEY MUST BE HIS PARENTS.
OH, HOW TOUCHING!
A SCENE OF FAMILY BLISS...
NOW WHAT..?
IS YOUR MOTHER ANGRY WITH US?
NO, WITH ME FOR BORROWING A FLYING SAUCER.

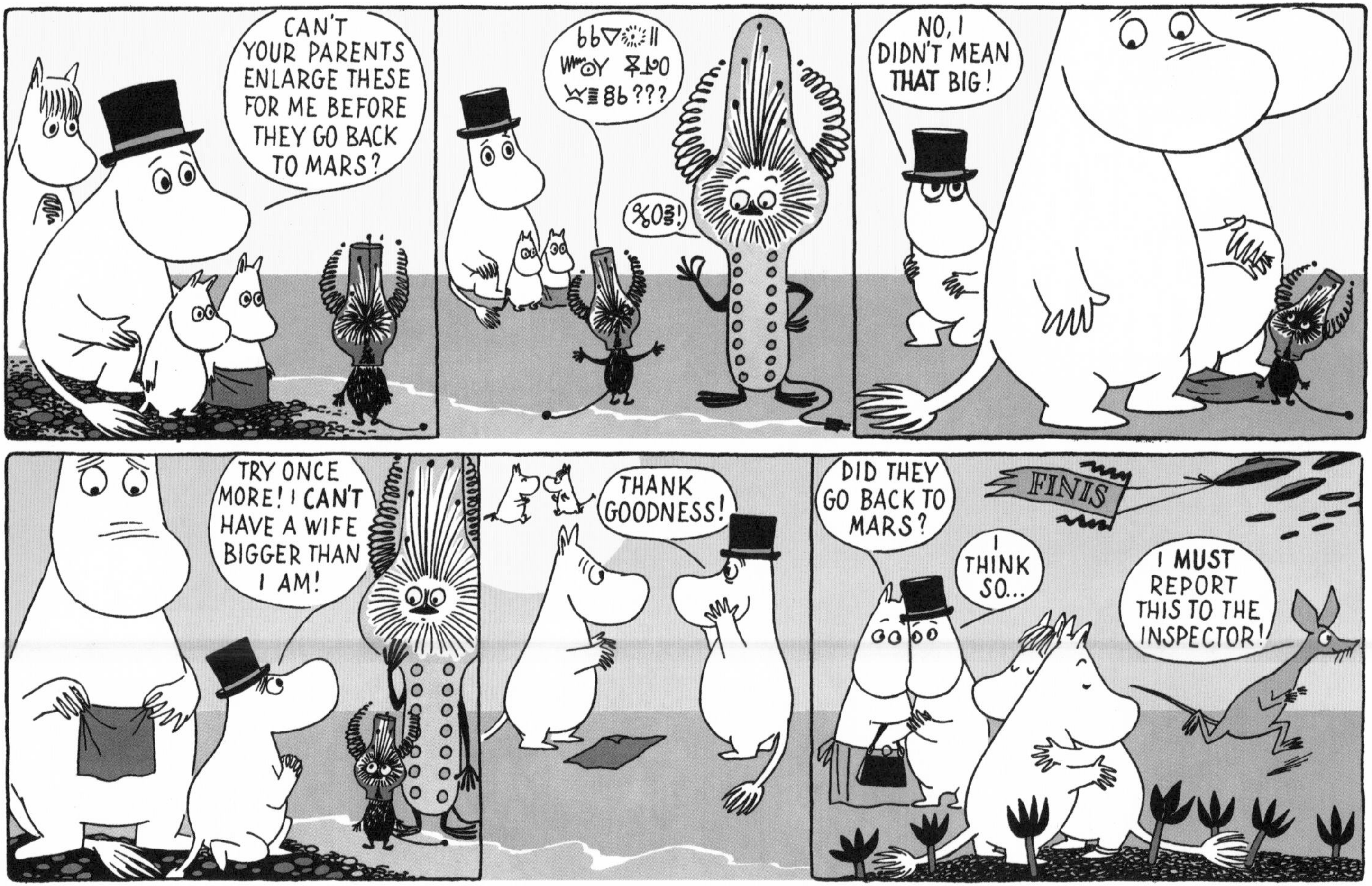
CAN'T YOUR PARENTS ENLARGE THESE FOR ME BEFORE THEY GO BACK TO MARS?
NO, I DIDN'T MEAN THAT BIG!
TRY ONCE MORE! I CAN'T HAVE A WIFE BIGGER THAN I AM!
THANK GOODNESS!
DID THEY GO BACK TO MARS?
I THINK SO...
FINIS
I MUST REPORT THIS TO THE INSPECTOR!

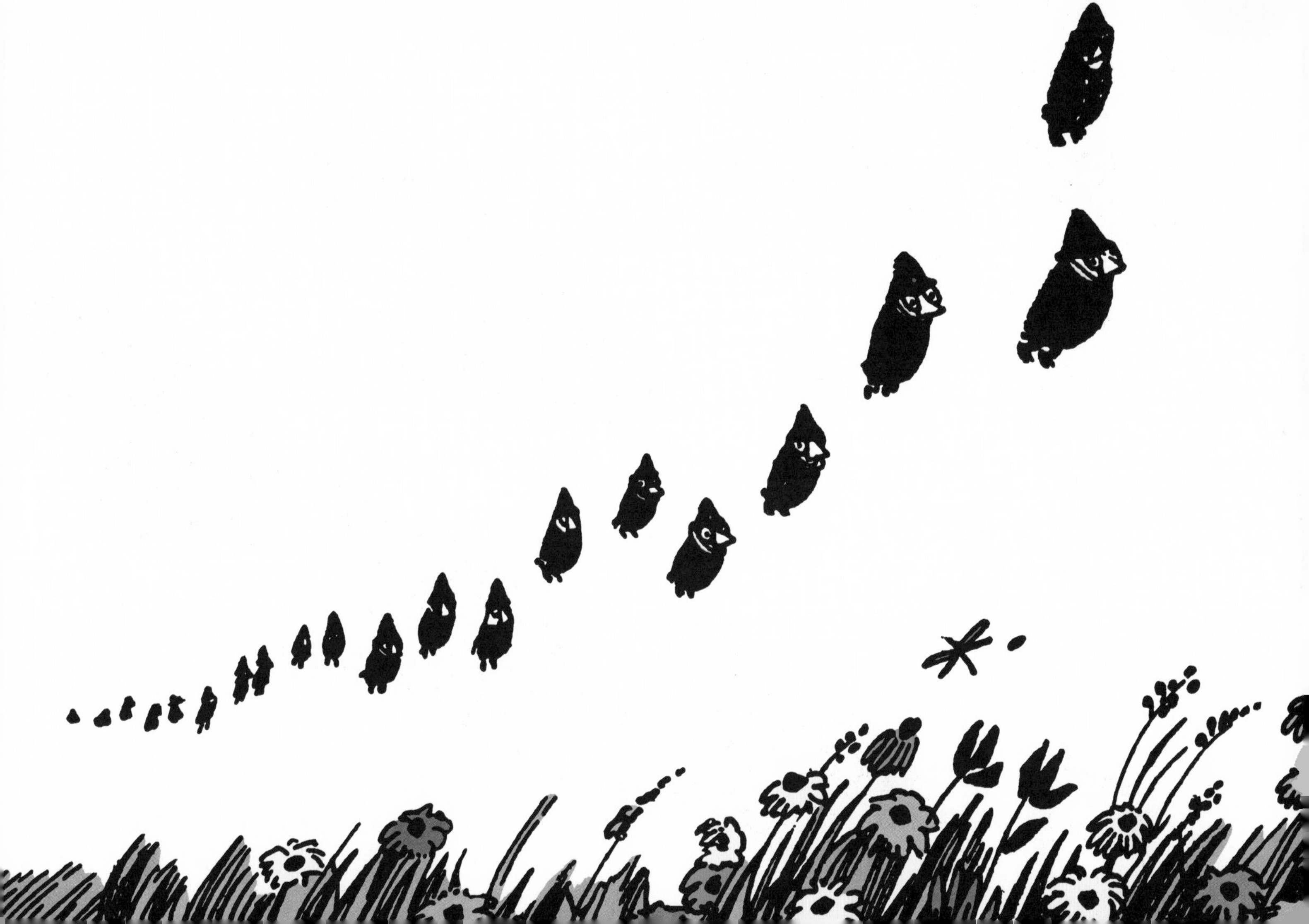

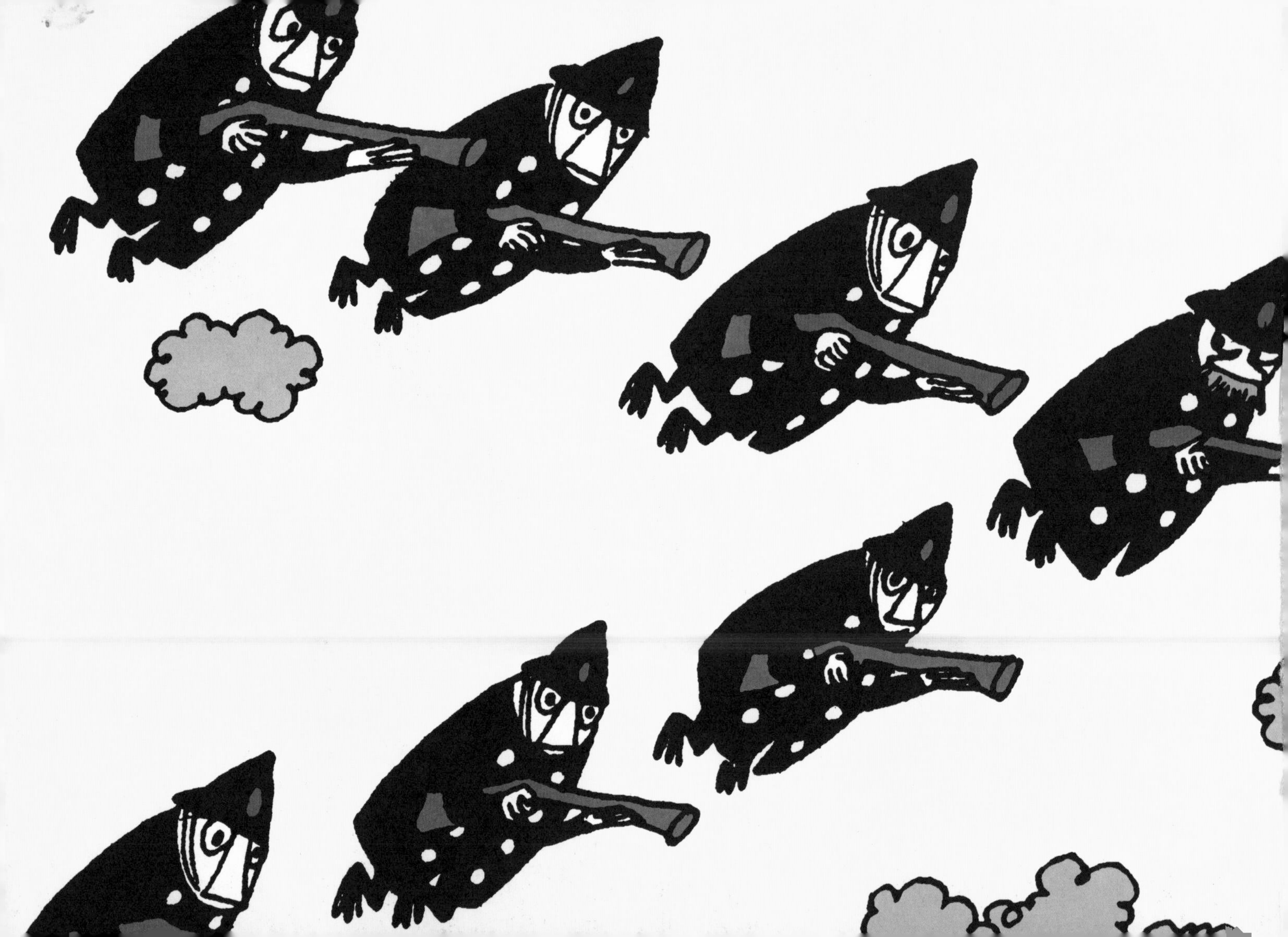

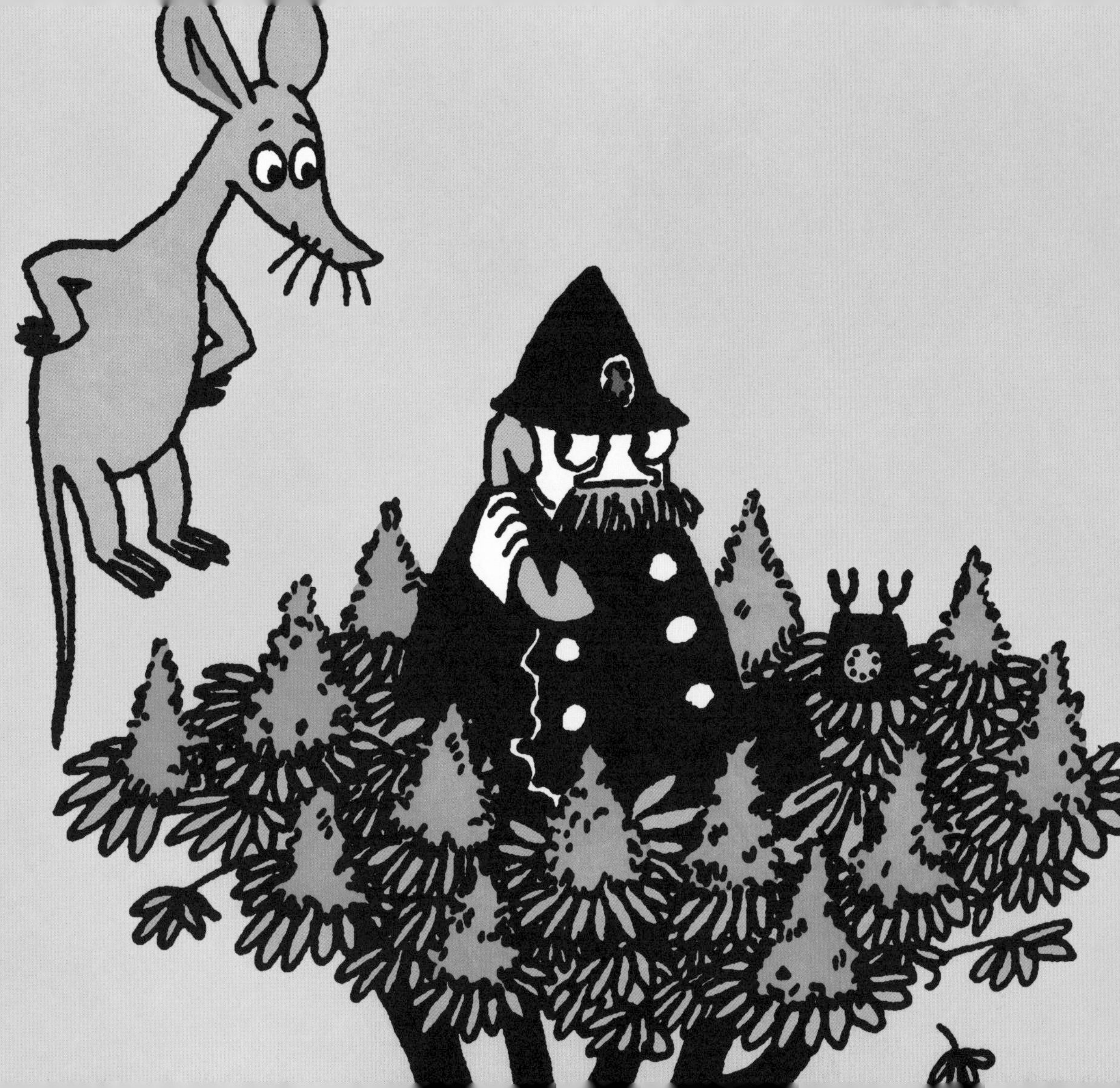

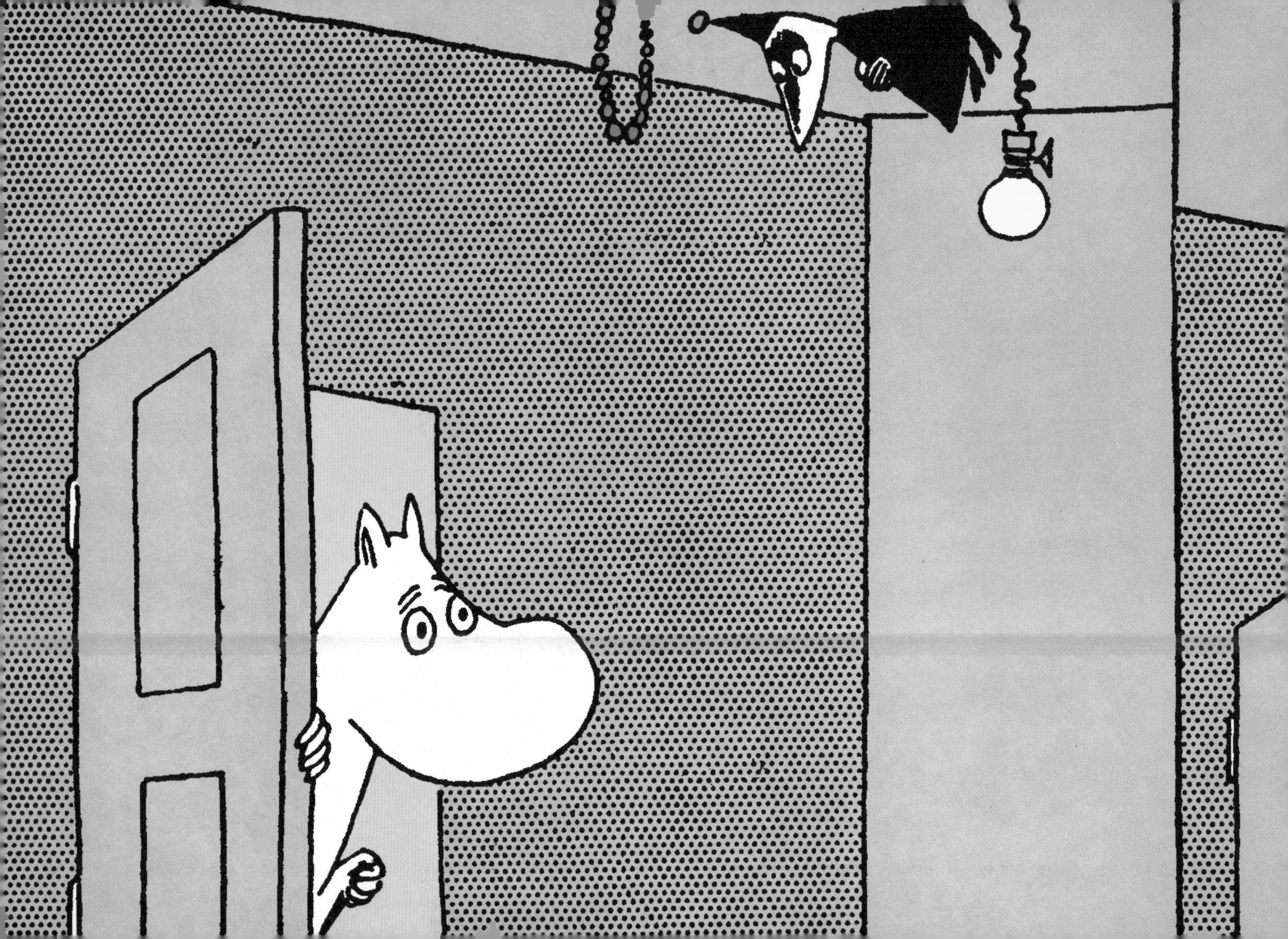